Miss Fiona's Fancy

Marion Chesney

A SIGNET BOOK
NEW AMERICAN LIBRARY

NAL BOOKS ARE AVAILABLE AT QUANTITY DISCOUNTS WHEN USED TO
PROMOTE PRODUCTS OR SERVICES. FOR INFORMATION PLEASE WRITE TO
PREMIUM MARKETING DIVISION, NEW AMERICAN LIBRARY,
1633 BROADWAY, NEW YORK, NEW YORK 10019

Copyright © 1987 by Marion Chesney

All rights reserved.

SIGNET TRADEMARK REG. U.S. PAT. OFF. AND FOREIGN COUNTRIES
REGISTERED TRADEMARK—MARCA REGISTRADA
HECHO EN CHICAGO, U.S.A.

SIGNET, SIGNET CLASSIC, MENTOR, ONYX, PLUME,
MERIDIAN and NAL BOOKS are published by NAL PENGUIN INC.,
1633 Broadway, New York, New York 10019

First Printing, July, 1987

1 2 3 4 5 6 7 8 9

PRINTED IN THE UNITED STATES OF AMERICA

Dancing with Disaster

"Miss Grant," Lady Bellamy said, "may I present the Marquess of Cleveden, who is desirous of dancing the waltz with you."

And for the first time, Fiona Grant stood face to face with the man she had so confidently wagered she would wrap around her little finger.

"Damned!" thought Fiona. "Damned, and doubled damned." Here was no faded gentleman past his prime who would be flattered by the attention of a young miss —here was quite the handsomest gentleman she had ever met, not to mention the wealthiest and clearly most self-confident.

Then he placed his hand firmly on her waist, and she knew that if she were to bring this man to his knees, she first had to find a way to keep from being swept off her feet....

SIGNET REGENCY ROMANCE (0451)

Follies of the Heart

- ☐ THE WOOD NYMPH by Mary Balogh (146506—$2.50)
- ☐ A CHANCE ENCOUNTER by Mary Balogh (140060—$2.50)
- ☐ THE DOUBLE WAGER by Mary Balogh (136179—$2.50)
- ☐ A MASKED DECEPTION by Mary Balogh (134052—$2.50)
- ☐ RED ROSE by Mary Balogh (141571—$2.50)
- ☐ THE TRYSTING PLACE by Mary Balogh (143000—$2.50)
- ☐ POOR RELATION by Marion Chesney (145917—$2.50)
- ☐ THE EDUCATION OF MISS PATTERSON by Marion Chesney (140052—$2.50)
- ☐ THE ORIGINAL MISS HONEYFORD by Marion Chesney (135660—$2.50)
- ☐ MARRIAGE MART by Norma Lee Clark (128168—$2.25)
- ☐ THE PERFECT MATCH by Norma Lee Clark (124839—$2.25)
- ☐ THE IMPULSIVE MISS PYMBROKE by Norma Lee Clark (132734—$2.50)
- ☐ CAPTAIN BLACK by Elizabeth Hewitt (131967—$2.50)
- ☐ MARRIAGE BY CONSENT by Elizabeth Hewitt (136152—$2.50)
- ☐ A SPORTING PROPOSITION by Elizabeth Hewitt (143515—$2.50)
- ☐ A MIND OF HER OWN by Anne McNeill (124820—$2.25)
- ☐ THE LUCKLESS ELOPEMENT by Dorothy Mack (129695—$2.25)
- ☐ THE BELEAGUERED LORD BOURNE by Michelle Kasey (140443—$2.50)

Prices slightly higher in Canada

Buy them at your local bookstore or use this convenient coupon for ordering.

NEW AMERICAN LIBRARY
P.O. Box 999, Bergenfield, New Jersey 07621

Please send me the books I have checked above. I am enclosing $_____
(please add $1.00 to this order to cover postage and handling). Send check
or money order—no cash or C.O.D.'s. Prices and numbers are subject to change
without notice.

Name_____

Address_____

City_____ State_____ Zip Code_____

Allow 4-6 weeks for delivery.
This offer is subject to withdrawal without notice.

*For Felicia Villiers
With love*

ONE

Although Walter Scott's poetry was just beginning to make the Highlands of Scotland a romantic place in the eyes of the *ton*, very few members of Regency society would dream of leaving their overheated saloons and clubs to go and see the place for themselves. And so most of them remained unaware that the Scottish aristocracy and gentry still lived in a manner alien to their English counterparts.

On the other hand, many members of the Scottish upper classes were familiar with the hectic London Season, making the long journey each year in the hopes of finding suitable husbands for their daughters.

But at least one daughter of the Scottish landed gentry remained, as yet, blissfully unaware of the competition, the snobbery, and the rigid social rules among English society. Her name was Fiona Grant, and she lived with her parents, Sir Edward and Lady Grant, in a large ancient mansion, Strathglass House, located some miles outside Inverness and surrounded by deep pine forests.

Fiona was very popular. She had an open, easy manner and was quite unaware of her great beauty. She had thick chestnut hair that burned with tiny fiery red lights like sparks from a peat fire on a frosty night. Her complexion was flawless and her wide eyes were very green—not hazel, but as green as a cat's.

The one great flaw in her personality was that she had inherited her father's addiction to gambling.

Sir Edward was a lawyer, having been brought up at a time when the French Revolution had caused tremors of fear to run through the British upper classes, and just in case Britain should follow the French example, he had, like many of his kind, been trained to a profession. Like Fiona, he was spared the hells of heavy gambling because of geographical circumstances. The only neighbors with any money were too far distant to make more than two or three calls a year and the servants and tenants were too poor. Fiona gambled with the maids, using paper spills for money, each spill representing one hundred guineas, while her father was often reduced to playing cards with Angus Robertson, his piper, for shillings, not a very rewarding pastime, for if he won, he had to pay the piper, and if he lost, Angus would merely disappear into the hills for a week until such time as he considered his master might have forgotten the debt.

The fact that the Grants could do with more money was evident in the style in which they lived. Very little had been done to modernize the mansion, and the kitchen was still a disgraceful building of turf tacked onto the back of the house with holes in the turf roof open to the sky to let the smoke out, for there was no chimney. One day a mouse had fallen off the rafters into the soup and Lady Grant had vowed to tear down the kitchen and build a new one, but nothing had come of it.

In the Highland manner, the Grants sheltered many dependents under their roof. Fiona's old nurse lived in the attics, along with her governess, and two housemaids, too old to continue in service. Then there were various relatives, such as two half-pay captains and three maiden aunts, who had come on a visit a long time ago and showed no signs of leaving.

Fiona loved her home. Having never lived anywhere else, apart from a brief childhood sojourn in an equally dilapidated house in Edinburgh, she saw no fault in it. She had been strictly brought up in her childhood but now had more freedom than any young lady of her class usually enjoyed.

She rode her shaggy Highland pony over the moors of her father's estate and through dark forests, so thick that the great gales of winter could not penetrate and cried far above her head in the tops of the pines with a dismal moaning sound. The terror of invasion by Napoleon had spread even to this remote part of the country, and Fiona rode out with her father on field days to inspect their own regiment of Highlanders. She made a brave figure dressed in a tartan petticoat, red jacket, gaudily laced, and with the same style of bonnet ornamented with feathers as her father wore.

Although the daughter of the house, she was still expected to help the servants with household chores, which is why, on a cold November afternoon, Fiona was down on her hands and knees on the floor of the banqueting hall, chalking out squares that would enable the dancers to keep in their sets. A ball to celebrate her nineteenth birthday was to be held there that very evening.

She was looking forward to her birthday ball with the same mild pleasure she had looked forward to all the others. Dreams of romance still did not trouble her sleep. The young men who were coming to the ball she had known all her life and thought of as friends rather than as beaux.

She coughed as she worked, for the great fire in the hall smoked abominably, but then it always did. Fiona sometimes wished her father would make some push to have the chimneys rebuilt, but she alone found the smoke a nuisance, Sir Edward and his staff considering peat smoke beneficial and a sure way of keeping diseases at bay—as if diseases were so many mosquitoes.

Fiona finished chalking the floor just as the wheezing chime of an old grandfather clock in the darker recesses of the hall reminded her it was time to change into her party clothes.

Snow was beginning to drift gently down outside as Fiona put on a white muslin gown, high-waisted in the latest manner. Sir Edward always made sure she wore the newest fashions, for he admired his daughter's beauty, although he and Lady Grant never told her so, feeling that compliments might make her vain.

Fiona arranged her hair in a simple style, put on a thin necklace of coral, and drew on a pair of kid gloves that were wrinkled up to the elbow. She thought the gloves would surely have looked better had they been smooth, but Sir Edward had assured her that wrinkled gloves were "all the crack."

From down below, she could hear the groan of the bagpipes and the scrape of fiddles as the orchestra tuned up.

She had spent a long time dressing, for her parents wanted her to make an appearance. She rose to her feet, shivering a little, for thin muslin was little protection against the icy drafts of Strathglass House, and made her way to the top of the staircase that led down to the banqueting hall.

She stood for a moment, looking down at the assembled guests, envying the serving maids and tenants' wives their wool dresses—but not their bare feet. Only the ladies of the upper classes wore shoes.

It was a motley assortment of guests gathered below under the smoke-blackened beams. Tenants and servants, keepers, shepherds, stalkers, and poor relations all mixed together happily without paying any attention to degrees of rank.

On a small platform at the end stood Angus Robertson, fronting the orchestra. Angus was resident piper to the Grants and would not do any manual work for fear of ruining his hands.

Fiona started to descend the stairs, and then she froze. All at once she had a premonition that this evening was going to be different, that something was going to happen to her that would change her whole life. An initial feeling of dread was followed by one of elation and exhilaration. She felt she was standing on the threshold of something momentous.

She took a deep breath and began to descend the stairs.

A cheer went up from the guests and servants when they saw her and she felt she was being engulfed in the great wave of love and goodwill that rose up to meet her.

Beaming proudly, her father led her into a set for the first reel. Fiona looked up at him, waiting for him to say something—something that would explain the odd feeling she had had at the top of the stairs—but he only smiled at her proudly and said, "You look cold, Fiona. A few reels will soon warm you."

Fiona danced and danced. For a while the feeling of anticipation left her. There was a rest from dancing at midnight when a great supper was served with everyone—servants, tenants, and aristocracy—sitting down together, the only social distinction being that whisky punch was served to the lower orders while wine was served to the gentry.

Sir Edward rose to make a speech and again Fiona felt that almost suffocating sensation of anticipation, but her father said nothing at all out of the way, merely delivering the same speech he had delivered on all her other birthdays.

At two in the morning, the dancing resumed and did not end until dawn, which arrived in the middle of the morning, as during the long Scottish winter the sun rises at ten and sets around two in the afternoon.

Standing wearily beside her parents, saying good-bye to the guests, Fiona became convinced that she had imagined her earlier feeling that something was about to happen.

Sir Edward went off to the library and Fiona was about to climb the stairs to her room when her mother beckoned her and told her that her father wanted to speak to her on a most important matter.

Fiona's heart began to beat quickly. All at once she was sure she knew what was going to happen. Her father had a marriage planned for her and that was what he wanted to discuss with her. The most likely candidate was Jamie Grant, a fourth cousin who had lands on the banks of Loch Ness. Jamie was well enough, thought Fiona ruefully, but the same age as herself and still at times more like a schoolboy than a man. And yet, if Jamie had been chosen for her, she was prepared to accept him.

But Jamie! Sulky, petulant Jamie! Surely all that feeling of excitement, that feeling something momentous was about to happen, should have been the herald of some event greater than the prospect of marriage to Jamie Grant.

Fiona sighed. If her father had chosen Jamie, then Jamie it would have to be. Fiona knew her father had always longed for a son and felt she had somehow let him down by being a mere girl. The least she could do was to accept the husband of his choice.

She followed her mother to the library, a large gloomy room with serried ranks of bookshelves rising high up to the blackened ceiling. Fiona did not have happy memories of this room. It was here she had point-blank refused to dust the bookshelves with a fox's tail when she was only eight years old. She dreaded the thought of climbing up the library steps with that fox's tail in her hand, sure that the ghost of a tailless fox would appear to bite her. Her rebellion had shocked her father. She had been locked in a dark cupboard beside the fire, where the peat was kept, and left there, sobbing with misery for a whole hour.

Sir Edward Grant was a tall thin man like a beanpole. He wore the kilt when he was at home, having never paid the slightest attention, even when it was being enforced, to that stupid English law that forbade the wearing of tartan in Scotland. He had not practiced his profession for some time but had frequently threatened to move to Edinburgh and start in business again. Although he studied all the latest developments in farming, he made disastrous and expensive mistakes. He had at one time purchased a piece of land in Hertfordshire in England. He had bought at great cost a large drove of fine black cattle in Moray with a view to driving them down to England and selling the beef on the London Market. But before his drovers set off south, he had told them to put the cattle in a small paddock between the orchard and the river bordered on the shrubbery side by a yew hedge. By next day, the poor beasts had eaten the hedge, and lay about the paddock, dead or dying from the effects of the poison.

Lady Grant, showing little weariness from the night's celebrations, sat down beside the fire and took out a piece of embroidery. She was a fat, placid woman who had never fallen out of love with her husband and found she could lead a comfortable life provided she agreed with everything he said.

"Fiona," said Sir Edward, speaking in English instead of Gaelic, a sure sign of the weightiness of the interview, "I have decided to remove to London and study for the English bar. We have need of money and there are no fat pickings to be had north of the border. English law, as you know, is different from Scottish law, but if I study hard, I am sure I can master its intricacies very quickly."

"And we are to go too?" asked Fiona. "To London?"

"Yes, and hope of finding a suitable husband for you is what forced me to make the move. There are plenty of fine men between Inverness and Edinburgh. But we need money, and if you made an advantageous English marriage, it would be the saving of us."

"We have also decided," said Lady Grant in her clear calm voice, "that keeping in mind we are relying on you to save our fortunes, you may marry whom you please—or rather, you will not be compelled to marry anyone you have taken in dislike."

A flash of humor lit Fiona's green eyes. "Of course, Mama," she said, "there are fortunes to be won at the gambling tables of St. James's."

"Aye," exclaimed Sir Edward, his eyes gleaming. "I kept that in mind. I have a quick mind and a deft way with the cards."

"Beware," mocked Fiona. "Playing hazard, dice, and whist with Angus the piper may not be the same thing as putting your lands in forfeit on a London card table."

"You must curb that unruly tongue of yours," said Lady Grant, putting a blue stitch neatly into a near-finished silk delphinium on her embroidery.

"Oh, leave her be," said Sir Edward good-humoredly. "There's plenty of fine London bucks who will like a girl with spirit."

"Quite so," said Lady Grant placidly, agreeing with him as usual.

Miss Fiona's Fancy

"But London is so very far away," said Fiona. "I did not like Edinburgh at all, and that is a capital city as well."

When her father was working as a lawyer in Edinburgh and Lady Grant had been in ill health, Fiona had been at the mercy of the Edinburgh servants. Her bath was a tin one, out in the backyard of the house. Every week it was filled with cold water, whether winter or summer, and Fiona, then eight, had been dragged screaming down from the nursery in the attics and plunged into the icy bath. If she would not eat anything at supper, it was presented to her at breakfast, and if refused, then at the following meal, until one day, faint from starvation, she was locked in a cupboard with a stodgy pudding she had refused for three days and told to stay there until she had eaten it. It was only when her feeble wails had penetrated the soft heart of a Highland chambermaid that the news of her plight was whispered to Lady Grant and she was released from her prison. It was not so much the bullying over the food that had angered Lady Grant, who had been brought up the same way, but the frequent baths, shocking in an age when washing all over was only recommended for medicinal purposes. And yet, despite the horror the cruelty of the servants had given Fiona for the whole of Edinburgh, she continued the ritual of the weekly bath when she was much older, for after having been clean, she found an unclean body uncomfortable.

"London is a grand place," said Sir Edward

dreamily. "We will arrive in time for the Season. There will be parties and routs and theaters. Lizzie Grant is apprenticed to a dressmaker in South Molton Street and will instruct you in all the latest fashions." Lizzie Grant was Sir Edward's brother's "accidental daughter," a polite Highland euphemism for an illegitimate female child. Sir Edward's eyes glowed as he talked, for he was privately thinking of the great fortune he was sure to make at the tables.

Lady Grant put one neat stitch after another in her embroidery and turned the names of their wealthier connections over in her mind. She was perfectly sure her husband would lose so much money that they would have to flee back to Scotland and was already preparing herself to approach various friends for money. But she accepted her husband's addiction to gambling as a Family Curse, something hereditary which nothing could be done about.

Fiona fell to thinking about marriage. She had already made up her mind she would have to marry *someone*. That was the way of the world. She hoped she would turn out like her mother and be able to tolerate some gentleman, faults and all. Fiona adored gambling as much as her father, but unlike him she could not face even her mythical losses of hundreds to some of the maids with equanimity. To repay her father for her having been born a mere girl, she must do her duty and go after the richest man at the Season. But he would possibly be English, she thought in dismay, and would expect her to live out the rest of her days in England. Perhaps, after all, there might be some way to get out of marriage. Perhaps she could contrive some way to win money for herself. She was luckier at cards and dice than her father.

Gradually her father stopped talking, his eyes bright with dreams of gaining a fortune at cards. Lady Grant stitched while she plotted and planned ways—although without any deep worry or anguish—to save them from debtors' prison, and Fiona gazed into the flickering flames of the peat fire and wondered who she would marry.

At last Sir Edward roused himself from his reverie and sent Fiona off to bed. But Fiona only went to her room to change into her riding habit before going round to the stables. She felt too excited to sleep. The crisp snow crunched under her pony's hooves and the mountains stood out sharp against the pale blue winter sky. When she was married—*if* she married—she might return one day. She *must* return one day to this, her beloved home. No thoughts of love or romance entered Fiona's practical mind. Her duty lay in seeing that her father retained Strathglass House and his lands. That he might easily have done so had he been a more sensible manager of his estates and less addicted to gambling did not occur to Fiona. She could well understand the lure of the tables, and farming was a treacherous business at the best of times.

A pair of golden eagles sailed high above. Fiona reined in her horse and watched them for a long time until her eyes blurred with tears and she could no longer see them. She was only dimly aware that she had been as free as the eagles and London was about to throw conventional chains around her from which she might never escape.

The harsh northern winter still held its grip on the land as the Grants set out on their journey to London three months later to arrive in time for the start of the Season in April.

A thin sleety drizzle was blowing across the moors as Fiona said farewell to her home. Many of the tenants and servants were openly crying while the cumbersome traveling carriage was harnessed to four powerful horses and laden with imperials, hatboxes, and a great hair trunk that had reminded Fiona when she was very little of the pictures of the American buffalo she had in her schoolbooks. Fiona and her parents and Christine, some other "accident" of the Grant family who had been elected lady's maid, were to travel together. A heavy post-chariot behind carried two maids and two footmen, a hamper of food, a spirit stove, and an entire tea service in case the Grants felt like refreshing themselves between posting houses and relatives' homes. Outside were the postilions, very fine in green jackets and jockey caps, riding the family horses; Fiona's pony, Blackie, was tied behind her father's horse.

Miss Fiona's Fancy

Angus, the piper, waited sulkily in the courtyard. He was to send them off and then ride after to join the party, for Sir Edward never went anywhere without his piper. Angus felt he should have been allowed to travel in the post-chariot and was grumbling openly about the damage the sleety weather might do to his hands.

But as the coachman cracked his whip, Angus tuned his pipes and began to play "Farewell to the North," a heartbreaking melody that reduced everyone to tears.

There must be Scottish lords in London, thought Fiona, miserably drying her eyes. "A husband who would love this place as much as I do would be worth all my devotion, all my loyalty," but she privately thought that such a man only existed in dreams.

It took them three days to reach Perth, where they stayed with her father's only surviving uncle, an Episcopal minister, Ian Grant. They traveled only thirty miles a day, stopping at inns on the road, going to bed early and rising late. Then they continued south until they got to the ferry at Inverkeithing. The short crossing to Queensferry took three hours; the sailing boat being a dirty, ugly, miserable vessel. When they reached Edinburgh, Fiona still saw the city with a jaundiced eye, seeing not the splendor of the buildings of the New Town but only the unsightly parks abandoned to squabbling washerwomen. She was glad that their stay—with another relative—was confined to a mere two days.

The later stops on the road to London became jumbled together, a relative's house here, a posting house there. Fiona had not realized she had quite so many relatives. Some lived in great comfort and some in little more than cottages. Then there was a week's stop at Scarborough, Sir Edward becoming convinced that Lady Grant was in need of sea bathing. Although sea bathing was approved of, Fiona found the English did not believe in baths, although quite a number of Scottish relatives had fallen under what was called "the French influence" and were even known to take baths *twice a day*. Fiona was astounded by the immensity of the sea at Scarborough and enjoyed wandering on the beach and exploring the caves. But all too soon it was time to leave. More posting houses, more inns, and London drawing ever nearer.

At her father's command, one evening on April 2, the carriage stopped at the top of Highgate Hill and they all got out to have a look at London.

It lay spread out below them, houses and churches lying crouched and threatening under a pall of smoke.

Fiona's heart sank. She climbed back into the carriage and tried not to cry. A wave of homesickness, so strong and so piercing, made her feel almost ill.

"I saw two magpies," said Sir Edward cheerfully as he climbed in after Fiona. "I am going to be lucky, I know it."

Lady Grant gave him a wan smile and Fiona sat very still, white and tense, thinking of that smoky, gloomy city below that was shortly about to swallow her up.

TWO

Lady Grant, who had enjoyed good health for some time, despite her husband's worries about her in Scarborough, fell victim to a bout of influenza as soon as they were settled in London. Instead of taking rooms in Lincoln's Inn Fields, which would have suited both his purse and his profession, Sir Edward rented a large house facing Rotten Row in Hyde Park.

At first he seemed determined to lead a sober life and traveled to the law courts each day to study and made no mention of gambling. With Lady Grant confined to bed, Fiona found herself leading a life oddly similar to her Highland one. She rode her pony, Blackie, in the Park, accompanied by the piper, Angus Robertson, who liked to appear beside her on one of her father's best horses, saying that since he had no opportunity to play the pipes, he may as well take his exercise. They made an odd couple, the lanky Highlander on the tall rawboned horse and pretty Fiona on her shaggy little pony. Many members of the Quality stopped to stare, but Fiona saw nothing odd in this, considering it a rather rude London fashion. Various relatives turned up to see Lady Grant, who was fast recovering, and the household had that odd, easygoing Highland atmosphere where the servants gossiped freely to their masters and often joined in games of charades in the evening or discussed the latest plays or books, all the Scottish servants having been well educated at the parish school. Although they had brought few servants with them, there had been no need to hire English ones. Word had got about that the Grants were in Town and Highlanders who had recently left the navy or army turned up on their doorstep looking for employment.

After a few weeks of this pleasant undemanding life, an old friend of Lady Grant, the Duchess of Gordonstoun, came to call. She was a tough energetic Scottish lady who had successfully married off two daughters. Fiona was paraded in front of her, rather like a horse, and the little duchess poked her and prodded her and scrutinized her and did everything but look at her teeth.

After her examination of Fiona, the duchess turned to Lady Grant, who was lying on a chaise longue in their shabby drawing room. The house had been previously tenanted by Lord Ecclesham, who had a large brood of children, and so all the furniture was kicked and scarred. "You had better puff her off soon, Annie," said the duchess, Annie being Lady Grant's first name, "or everyone will be stealing a march on you. Can she dance?"

"I . . ." began Fiona, but the duchess raised an imperious hand to silence her.

"I was addressing your mother, child," she said.

"She has been well taught by Mr. Forsyth of Inverness," said Lady Grant.

"Be sure she knows the English way of dancing," said the duchess, "and don't have her leaping about the ballroom like a savage. Have you ordered her wardrobe?"

"I haven't been well enough to do anything, Betty," said Lady Grant, one of the few people allowed to address the duchess on familiar terms. "We have someone, a sort of relative, who is apprenticed to the Misses Hatton of South Molton Street—Lizzie Grant."

"Then we must send for her right away. Goodness, when I think of the eligibles in Town, and a beauty like this being hidden away! Get your bonnet, child. We may as well start by visiting the shops. Don't send for this Lizzie. I shall take Fiona to South Molton Street myself."

Once in the carriage with the Duchess of Gordonstoun, Fiona tried to make conversation but found all her sallies rudely snubbed. The duchess often said she never wasted her time talking or listening to any female under thirty years because they had heads filled with rubbish.

Fiona was too excited to be out and about to be offended. Their first call was at Green's, the glovers, in Little Newport Street. Fiona's whole attention, however, was caught by the shop next door to the glovers which sold nothing but dolls. A special clockwork device had been placed in the window to rock a doll backward and forward, showing that its eyes could open and shut. Fiona stood openmouthed, watching this miracle, until the duchess testily told her not to behave like a rustic and dragged her into the glovers. After having purchased calico gloves and kid gloves for Fiona and having charged them to Lady Grant, the duchess then swept her off to Rundell & Bridge, the jewelers, where the duchess had left a necklace to be cleaned. At first sight, Fiona could not believe this was the most famous jewelers in the world because the outside was disgracefully shabby and dirty. But inside it was like a fairy palace with necklaces, tiaras, parures, and brooches sending flashing prisms of light stabbing through the gloom of the shop. A man was filling a scoop with small brown-looking stones. Fiona asked him what he was doing and he said he was "shoveling in rubies." Fiona caught her breath in delight.

Then to the Misses Hatton in South Molton Street. It was the day before one of the court days at the Queen's House and room after room was filled with great whalebone hoops, as the simple high-waisted fashions of the Regency were still forbidden at royal receptions. The hoops were great circles of whalebone, covered with silk and then with lace and net and hung about with festoons of lace and beads, garlands of artificial flowers, and furbelows of all sorts. Then there were the headdresses to go with these magnificent "bodies," some of them consisting of as many as twelve feathers, standing bolt upright, and forming a forest of plumage. The train that went with these court gowns was very narrow, more like a prolonged sash than a garment. Fiona was studying the hoops and wondering how anyone could possibly move in such a tenue when one of the Miss Hattons summoned her to their saloon for tea and cakes and flattery. Fiona felt she had been silent for so long that when she spoke her voice would come out cracked and squeaky and was therefore relieved to find herself boldly asking after Lizzie Grant.

Lizzie was summoned. Fiona looked at her Grant relative curiously. She was not at all like a Grant in appearance. She was small and plump and dainty and had a rather disconcerting way of never meeting your eyes direct, but always looking at some point just to the side of your face. With her usual open friendliness, Fiona started to address Lizzie in Gaelic, but Lizzie did not, or pretended not, to understand, but the duchess most certainly did, and reprimanded Fiona sternly for speaking in a "foreign tongue," as if Gaelic were the language of some country other than her own. While the duchess was berating her, Fiona had an uneasy feeling that Lizzie was enjoying the tirade, although she stood there meekly with her hands folded. "You could learn some manners from Lizzie here," ended the duchess. "*She* is always prettily behaved."

The measuring and fittings began. All Fiona's clothes were chosen by Lizzie, who appeared to be a great favorite, not only with her employers, but also with the Duchess of Gordonstoun.

Fiona found she herself was becoming prey to an alarming wish to sulk. But she could find no fault in the fashions Lizzie chose for her. The colors were flattering and the styles were simple and elegant.

Not used to disliking people, Fiona found she was beginning to detest Lizzie although, she did not know quite why, and was relieved when the visit was at last over. Then they went to Churton's for stockings and on to Ross to buy wigs for the duchess. Every woman past the first bloom of youth wore an expensive wig instead of her own hair. Fiona was beginning to be heartily tired of shopping, but a visit to Lowe for shoes was still to be endured—and then came the highlight of the outing. The duchess ordered her carriage to drive them to St. Paul's Churchyard to look at books, and Fiona spent a happy hour rummaging among the bookstalls.

For a few days afterward, life sank back to its quiet rhythm, but Lady Grant, fully recovered and determined to do her duty by her daughter, began to "nurse the ground"—as the entertaining of the parents of eligible young men was called.

There seemed to be endless calls and card

leavings and endless tea parties. Again, as with the duchess, Fiona found she was expected to sit quietly and listen while she and her marriage prospects were discussed. Fiona's only comfort was that her mother appeared to worry that Sir Edward no longer went to the law courts but had had himself elected to Brooks's in St. James's where he went nightly, and came home at dawn, sometimes hysterically elated, sometimes gray and drawn.

Her new wardrobe was delivered and completed. Fiona hoped not to see Lizzie Grant for some time, but the Duchess of Gordonstoun arrived one afternoon to say she had a mind to take "little Fiona" to one of the Hanover Square Concerts, and that she had invited Lizzie Grant as well because it was a shame such a pretty biddable girl should spend all her days slaving in a workroom. Fiona herself thought it unfair, too, that Lizzie, because of an accident of birth, should be condemned to earn her bread, but she could not help wishing the duchess had not invited her as well.

Lizzie was shy and deferential and polite to Fiona as they set out and Fiona heartily wished she could find it in her to like this relative.

The Hanover Square Concerts were famous. They boasted all the best singers: Bartleman, Braham, Kelly, the Knyvetts, Mr. and Mrs. Vaughan, Mrs. Bianchi, and Mrs. Billington.

It was when Mrs. Billington, accompanied on the violin by the great Salomon, sang Handel's

"Sweet Bird that Shunn'st the Noise of Folly," that Fiona disgraced herself. For in London, to show any excess of emotion *was* a disgrace. But she had never heard sounds so sweet or so heart-wrenching. A picture of her Highland home rose in her mind's eye and her eyes filled with tears. The duchess was sitting between Lizzie and Fiona, and Fiona's emotion might have passed unobserved, had not Lizzie, who had been leaning forward a little with her chin on her hand, given Fiona one of her sideways glances and then whispered to the duchess, "Your grace, I fear Miss Grant is overcome."

"Behave yourself this minute," hissed the duchess angrily to Fiona.

Fiona glanced about the room, looking for something to take her mind away from the beauty of the performance.

And then she found it.

A tall man was leaning against one of the pillars with his arms folded. He had a harsh, strong, handsome face, and thick black hair. He had a most odd color of eyes, thought Fiona, agate-colored, almost yellow, like a hawk, or like the eyes of those golden eagles at Strathglass. They wore a clouded, hooded, brooding expression as he listened to the music, and then, as if aware of her glance, the heavy lids raised and he stared at her. At first the glance was hard and predatory, and then a smile lifted the corners of his firm mouth and his eyes gleamed with humor.

Fiona blushed furiously for the first time in her

life and looked down at her hands, determined all at once to appear as meek and biddable as Lizzie.

But the duchess, who only attended the concerts because they were fashionable and was quite tone deaf, had not been caught up in the music and noticed the exchange of glances.

Nothing at all was said. Lizzie was taken back to South Molton Street, and then Fiona was taken home. She had quite recovered and did not find the duchess's silence odd since the duchess usually barely spoke to her anyway. But once they had reached the Grants' house, the Duchess of Gordonstoun announced her intention of going inside to speak to Lady Grant.

It was unfortunate for Fiona that her father had arrived home early after having lost heavily at the tables and was on hand to hear the Duchess of Gordonstoun complaining that Fiona was already losing her chances of making a rich marriage by *showing emotion* and *locking glances with some gentleman.* "So," finished the duchess, pausing to take a pinch of snuff, "I suggest you take that nice Lizzie Grant out of South Molton Street and make her a companion to your daughter."

Oh, no you don't, thought Fiona confidently. She knew she could protest and that her parents would listen. Sir Edward and Lady Grant had seen to it that Fiona was reared very strictly until her sixteenth birthday. After that, they considered her an adult and allowed her all the freedom she had so long craved.

"Papa," said Fiona with a smile, "I have no need

of a companion. The music was so very beautiful that I was temporarily overset. It will not happen again. I looked at the gentleman by accident when I was trying to compose myself. A trifling mistake. There is, furthermore, something about Lizzie I cannot like..."

Her voice trailed away. For once her father was not paying her the slightest attention. He was gazing eagerly, almost greedily, at the Duchess of Gordonstoun.

"Are you sure," he asked, "that Fiona could attract a rich fortune? It all seemed possible while we were still in Strathglass, but London is full of pretty girls who are also blessed with good dowries."

"If you let me take her about the Season at first," said the duchess, "and if you let Lizzie set her an example, then I am sure Fiona will 'take' very well."

"I am sure Mama is all I need as chaperone," said Fiona hotly, but her parents were looking hopefully at the duchess. Lady Grant knew her husband had dipped deep at the tables. He had lost money before, but always in Scotland to a friend or neighbor to whom one could appeal for a certain length of time to settle the account.

But only Sir Edward knew the exact extent of his losses. He owed Lord Alvanley £15,000— and unless Fiona's prospects were good, he had nothing but his home and his lands to offer the moneylenders by way of security. He avoided Fiona's angry gaze, and said, "That would be very kind of you. A good marriage is just what this family needs."

Fiona bit her lip and decided to hold her tongue until the formidable duchess had left. But no sooner had the Duchess of Gordonstoun fussed out into the night and Fiona immediately began to put her case than she realized her parents had hardened themselves against her pleas for the first time. It was evident to Lady Grant that Fiona was her husband's last hope. And much as she loved her only child, Sir Edward, as always, came first in her affections.

With unusual harshness, Lady Grant silenced her daughter by telling her not to be such a silly chit and sent her to bed.

Fiona lay awake for a long time, furious. It was not the fact that her parents expected her to make a good marriage that hurt—she would have found it strange had they expected less of her—it was that they had surrendered her up to the care of the Duchess of Gordonstoun and to Lizzie Grant. If only I could gamble like Papa, thought Fiona miserably. I am sure I would be lucky. There are gambling clubs for women, but unmarried girls like myself do not get elected and no gambling lady of the *ton* would dream of accepting my IOUs and I have no money with which to play cards or dice.

The door of the bedroom quietly opened and Christine Grant, the maid, came in. "I saw your candle burning," she said softly, "and wondered whether I could fetch you something."

Fiona struggled up against the pillows and looked curiously at this other accidental Grant daughter. These "accidental" offspring were a normal feature of Highland life and Fiona realized with a start she had never bothered to wonder about the fathers of these half-relatives.

Christine, unlike Lizzie, looked very Highland. She had masses of dark hair, a creamy skin, and steady gray eyes.

"Christine," said Fiona, "do you know Lizzie Grant?"

"Her what works i' the dressmakers? I saw her but once."

"Whose child is she?"

"Your uncle's. Sir Edward's brother, Charles, over at Aviemore."

Fiona wondered why she had not made the connection before. Lord Charles Grant was plump and fair and no more like the other members of the clan than his illegitimate daughter.

"And the mother?"

"I do not know, miss. 'Tis the same in my own case. Most grand families give the lassies a pension to bring up the child, but the Grants always took the child away after it was born into their own household."

"Who is your own father, Christine?" asked Fiona, and then wondered with a stab of fear whether Christine might prove to be her own half-sister.

"Thomas Grant of Speyside."

"And was he kind to you?"

"I never saw him. I was brought up and schooled with his own daughters and then when I was old enough I was sent as a servant to Sir Edward's household."

"Did that not strike you as hard?" asked Fiona. "To be educated as a lady and condemned to be a servant?"

"Oh, no." Christine smiled lazily in her usual amiable way. "I always knew what I was, a bastard. I would have had a dismal time of it most other places. I have cause to be grateful to the Grants."

"But don't you often wonder about your mother?"

Christine laughed and settled herself comfortably on the end of Fiona's bed. "I'll tell you a secret, miss. I know who my mother is. You can't keep a thing quiet in the Highlands. She's Jessie Blythe, one of the fishwives at the Helvendale market in Cromarty. I'm just one of many by different fathers. She's a bold coarse woman who's overfond of the whisky. It's better this way."

"And what of Lizzie? If everyone knows everything, surely people know the identity of her mother."

"No, that's the odd thing," said Christine, "there's never been a word about that. Lord Charles rode off one day and came back carrying the baby. He would not even tell his lady where he got Lizzie and who by."

Fiona sighed. "Marriage does seem to be a dreary affair, Christine."

"Only for the upper set," said Christine cheerfully. "I shall wed a Highlander of my own station and he will be loyal to me. Is that what troubles you, miss . . . marriage?"

Fiona sat up and hugged her knees. "It's like this, Christine. The Duchess of Gordonstoun is to have the launching of me and she has said that Lizzie Grant is to be my companion."

"And Sir Edward and my lady agreed?"

"Yes. I fear Papa is gambling again, and they need me to make a rich marriage."

"Oh, with your appearance you'll have no trouble at all," said Christine. "Pay this Lizzie no heed. Once you are suitably engaged, you can get rid of her."

"It may seem very odd," said Fiona cautiously, "but I would rather not *have* to marry. I am much luckier at cards than Papa. If only I could gamble!"

"It's different I should think," said Christine, "playing cards for mountains of guineas instead of playing with me for imaginary money. Besides, I hear tell that in the ladies' clubs, they mark the cards."

"Oh, if only I could go home," said Fiona wretchedly. "If only I had not been born a woman."

Christine reached behind her and plumped up Fiona's pillows. "Don't fret, Miss Fiona," she said. "Look at it this way—marriage is a lottery, and an amazing amount of young ladies win the prize, love *and* money."

"Love? Does it exist outside books?"

"Oh, yes, miss, indeed it does."

"And how do *you* know, Christine? Are you in love?"

"That's enough, miss," said Christine. "You ask too many questions. Now, what can I get you to settle you for the night?"

"I don't know," said Fiona. "I don't think anything can settle me this night. Oh, I know. Look in the drawer over there and you'll find a pack of cards. We'll play for hundreds and hundreds of guineas, just as if we were rich ladies."

"Very well, miss," said Christine. "But don't keep me awake all night!"

So Christine and Fiona forgot their troubles as they gambled by candlelight on top of the bedcover, laughing and teasing each other like old friends.

Only once during the night did Fiona remember that handsome man who had been the unwitting cause of bringing Lizzie Grant closer into her life. But she shrugged and thought with all the superstition of the true gambler that the gentleman was one of those people like black cats that one should never allow to cross one's path.

THREE

Despite her addiction to gambling, Fiona was a levelheaded girl.

She awoke late the next day, determined to do her best for the Grant family, even if that best meant enduring the chaperonage of the Duchess of Gordonstoun and Lizzie Grant.

Lizzie moved in. She was very quiet, always sewing something or knitting or tatting. She had very little conversation, but such as she had took the form of humbly chiding Fiona when she thought Miss Grant was too forward and bold.

Fiona contrived to rub along very well with Lizzie by paying her scant attention. When not out and about, Lizzie spent her time reading to Lady Grant and soon became popular with that undemanding lady.

After attending the playhouse, the opera, and several concerts, Fiona began to become acquainted with some of the other debutantes. It was not as if she could be really friendly with any of them, she thought sadly. They were all preparing for one thing, to find a husband during the Season, and were wary of a beauty like Fiona Grant. Each saw in the other debutante a possible rival. But Fiona became something of a favorite with them—as much as they could make a favorite of any pretty rival. Her open friendliness and unaffected gaiety drew them to her.

The Duchess of Gordonstoun had told Fiona that as morals were very strict in the *ton*, she must never reveal poor Lizzie's bastard status, but always refer to her as "cousin." Fiona goodnaturedly agreed, for much as she disliked Lizzie, she felt sorry for the girl for having been born out of wedlock.

Through listening to gossip, Fiona put together a list of the most eligible men in London. Although many gentlemen had already appeared to be attracted to her, she could not be quite sure how popular she was going to be with them until her first London ball. That would be the acid test.

Her gambling fever was now dormant. The strain on her father's face showed the Grant family fortunes were still at low ebb. Fiona began to wish her father had a less expensive Family Curse, like drunkenness or a passion for collecting objets d'art.

By the eve of her first ball, Fiona had become accustomed to the duchess's hectoring ways and Lizzie's meek and sly looks.

She felt she was going into battle. All the calls

and concerts and chatter had been mere military training.

The first setback came when Christine took her ball gown, only arrived that day from the Misses Hatton, from its tissue paper and exclaimed in dismay.

Fiona, sitting at her toilet table brushing her hair, said over her shoulder, "What is the matter, Christine?"

"I think they've sent the wrong gown," said Christine. "Only look. It's *red*!"

Fiona swung around on her stool. Christine shook out the gown and held it up.

It was of red silk, flaming red, uncompromising red.

Fiona got up and surveyed the line, the low neckline, the puffed sleeves, and the deep flounces.

"The style is the same as Lizzie chose for me," said Fiona, "but it was to be white muslin, not red silk. Go and ask Lizzie what happened."

Christine disappeared, only to return some ten minutes later looking puzzled. "Lizzie is already dressed and belowstairs with her grace. I tried to tell them about the gown being an unsuitable color, but her grace snapped at me—you know how she does, 'If Lizzie chose it, then Fiona may be assured it is in perfect taste.' I don't understand it. All the other debutantes will be in pastel colors or white. Lizzie is wearing the finest white muslin gown you've ever seen."

Fiona sighed. "Put it on me, Christine, and let us see how it looks. But I have red lights in my hair, and I do think the effect is going to be quite awful."

Christine helped her into the gown and then stood back while Fiona went to the long mirror to see the result.

"Oh, miss," said Christine, "you look beautiful, but, well, like one of those *dangerous* women."

"You mean I look like a tart," said Fiona. The gown was wickedly seductive. It clung to her body, showing off her deep-bosomed figure. Fiona felt she did not look like herself, but like someone more worldly and sophisticated. It was a pleasurable feeling, like finding a mask to hide behind, a role to play. "You know, Christine," said Fiona meditatively, "I feel Lizzie made the mistake deliberately. I think she meant me to look dreadful. If that is the case and the duchess is shocked, it may be the means of removing her from my house. On the other hand, I do not wish to destroy my chances. Can we make this ensemble a little more *jeune fille*, do you think?"

Christine put her head on one side, and then said, "It is quite correct for young ladies to wear flowers in their hair. Your mama has a set of very pretty white silk flowers, very tiny, like jasmine. I could make a garland for your hair."

"The very thing. Quickly. We will be late if we take much longer."

If the duchess had seen the full glory of Fiona's gown before they left the Grant mansion, then Fiona would most certainly have been ordered to change it. And that, thought Fiona, as she arrived downstairs with her gown covered by a cloak, was surely what Lizzie intended. But then, Lizzie would get the blame. So why?

Lizzie's eyes fastened for a moment on the ethereal coronet of jasmine decorating Fiona's thick chestnut hair. She cast her eyes down and opened her pale lips. But before she could speak, the duchess said, "Vastly pretty, those flowers. Lizzie can be trusted to produce the best effect."

Fiona looked cynically at Lizzie, waiting to see if she would stand there and meekly take the praise for something that had been Christine's idea, and that is just what Lizzie did.

The ball was being given by Lord and Lady Bellamy at their town house in Park Lane. Unlike most of the other town houses, which were quite small—the aristocracy not wishing to waste money on accommodation for only a few months of the year—the Bellamy home was vast and had a real ballroom instead of one improvised out of a chain of saloons.

The ladies were ushered into an anteroom to leave their cloaks. The duchess only had a shawl, which she handed to a maid and left the room, saying she would meet the girls in the hall. And so she still had not seen Fiona's red gown.

Lizzie patted her hair in the mirror and said in a whisper, "I had better join her grace. Do not be long, Fiona. It is not good manners to keep people waiting," and then sidled off.

Fiona sent a horrible scowl after her retreating back, and then sat down at one of the mirrors and poked a stray curl back into place.

She was immediately surrounded by some of the debutantes she had already met, all exclaiming over her gown and telling her she was "too vastly *daring* for words!"

"Oh, since we all have to get married," said Fiona, "I may as well make my mark at this first ball." She fished in her reticule and brought out her list of eligibles. "See!" she said, holding it up. "I am well prepared. Do but look and tell me if I have missed anyone."

Three of the girls came forward, put their heads together and studied the list. There was little Miss Euphemia Perkins, only sixteen and surely too young to have a Season. There was Lady Penelope Yarwood, harsh-faced and horsy, but already engaged to Colonel Henry Buxtable of the Blues. And there was plain Letitia Helmsdale who was rumored to be the richest heiress in London.

"Oh," squeaked Miss Perkins. "You have forgot the Marquess of Cleveden."

"Yes," boomed Lady Yarwood. "Can't ignore him."

"There's no hope there," said Miss Helmsdale, shaking her corkscrew curls. "He's thirty-seven, he's never married, and he's never even been in love!"

"Pooh! Must I chase an *old* man?" mocked Fiona.

"He's so handsome," sighed Miss Perkins. "But

I would bet any money in the world that he would never marry."

"You would?" Fiona sat up straight, her eyes gleaming. Here were three rich young ladies. All her gambling fever came roaring back. Surely a man as old as thirty-seven would be an easy target. When they were as old as that, thought Fiona naively, all they wanted was a pretty girl to sit and listen to all their boring old reminiscences. Various elderly gentlemen had already fallen over themselves trying to scrape an acquaintance with her when she rode in the Park. It wasn't like going after a *young* man.

"I bet you," said Fiona Grant, "I can get this Marquess of Cleveden to propose to me before the Season is over."

Lady Yarwood laughed. "How much?" she asked curiously.

Fiona took a deep breath. "Three thousand pounds," she said slowly.

"Let me see," said Miss Perkins, amazed. "If he proposes to you, we each pay you three thousand pounds. If he does not, then *you* must pay *us* three thousand each."

Fiona ignored the alarm bells screaming in her head.

"Yes," she said.

Miss Perkins began to giggle. "You know, Fiona —I may call you that, may I not?—you are *such* fun. I have plenty of money of my own, so I say yes."

"Like taking money from a child," said Lady Yarwood. "Oh, well, Fiona, the bet is on."

"I'll bet as well," squeaked Miss Helmsdale, quite white with excitement. "And I thought this Season was going to be dreadfully dull!"

They called for the maids to hurry off and find them a blank notebook so that they could enter their bets. The bet was dully logged as "Miss Fiona's Fancy." They were all laughing and teasing Fiona about her prospects when Fiona suddenly noticed Lizzie, standing behind the group, listening avidly.

"How long have you been standing there?" demanded Fiona.

"Only a moment," said Lizzie. "Her grace is furious at being kept waiting."

Fiona said good-bye to the others, Lady Yarwood gave the betting book to her own maid for safekeeping, and following Lizzie's drooping white muslin shoulders, Fiona joined the duchess in the hall.

"Good heavens, child!" cried the Duchess of Gordonstoun, appalled. "You cannot appear wearing *red!* Whatever possessed you, you wicked girl?"

"It was all dear little Lizzie's idea," said Fiona, indulging in what she considered a well-deserved burst of malice.

Lizzie burst into tears. She never did . . . she wouldn't . . . how could Fiona be so cruel . . . was it because she, poor Lizzie, was only a love child?

"It is no use trying to blame Lizzie," said the duchess. "You horrible unfeeling girl. As it is, I would have to take you home had not Lizzie had that brilliant idea of the headdress which makes the rest bearable."

"I am *not* a liar," flamed Fiona. She rounded on Lizzie. "I'll deal with you later, you sneaky little worm."

"Apologize to Lizzie this moment," said the duchess, "or I shall take you home." Fiona closed her lips in a mutinous line. She was just about to say she would never apologize to Lizzie when she remembered that bet. Everything hung on it. If she could only become engaged to the Marquess of Cleveden, then she could pay her father's debts, break her engagement, and persuade her grateful parents to take her back to Scotland.

"Perhaps I was a little harsh," said Fiona sweetly. "You see, your grace, if you question Christine Grant, you will find she made this headdress from some silk flowers of mama's. I was angry because Lizzie appeared to be taking praise for something Christine did. And this headdress was none of your doing, now, was it, Lizzie?"

Lizzie remained silent. "We have only to ask Christine," said Fiona softly.

The Duchess of Gordonstoun looked impatiently at Lizzie. "Well?" she demanded.

"The headdress was not my idea," whispered Lizzie in a broken little voice. "But I try so hard to please Fiona and nothing seems to work. I craved only a little praise. It was wrong of me. Forgive me."

Fiona waited to see how Lizzie enjoyed being on the receiving end of a tongue-lashing for a change, but to her amazement, the duchess said gruffly, "Now, child, there is no need to cry. Your situation is indeed a painful one and Fiona is not the easiest of girls to school. Come along. We have wasted enough time."

Perhaps I *am* being unfair, thought Fiona, as she mounted the staircase beside Lizzie. She looks almost brokenhearted and yet I could swear it was all an act.

She curtsied to Lady Bellamy and followed the duchess into the ballroom, blinking in the glare of light from hundreds of candles. Fiona tried not to stare. She had never been in anyone's home before where they could afford such an amount of light. When she had imagined the ballroom, she had envisaged it as having shadowy corners where she could go and hide should she prove to be a wallflower. But if she failed to "take," then she would be sitting there for all to see.

A quadrille was in progress. Lizzie and Fiona sat down on either side of the duchess. Fiona waited nervously. What if no one asked her to dance?

She looked toward the entrance where two men were just arriving and her heart sank. For one of them was the tall, handsome man with the yellow eyes, and superstitious Fiona felt her evening was doomed.

The dance finished. Lord Bellamy, a small, tubby man, came up to the duchess leading a gangling, blushing young man behind him. He presented the young man as Captain Rogers, who, he said, was just itching to dance. The captain stood with his shoulders drooping, looking down at his dancing pumps, and obviously wished the floor would open and swallow him.

Fiona and Lizzie were introduced. The captain raised his eyes and looked hopefully at Lizzie, for he was terrified in case he would have to lead the dazzler in the flaming dress onto the floor. But Lord Bellamy specialized in choosing partners for the shy young men at his balls, and so the captain was ordered to take Miss Fiona Grant onto the floor.

Now, the small orchestra was that famous one from Almack's Assembly Rooms, Neil Gow and his fiddlers from Edinburgh. The next dance was announced as a Sean Trews. Fiona smiled with delight. It was one of her favorites and she was surprised it was to be performed at this stately ball. The Sean Trews was a dance, created after Culloden, when the Highlanders were forbidden to wear the kilt, and the dance, rather like a Highland fling, was supposed to show the Highlander trying to kick off the offending English trews or trousers. Fiona did not realize that although Scottish reels were danced everywhere in London, the steps were a sedate watered-down version that turned them more into English country dances than high-springing wild Scottish ones. Neil Gow and his men played with great verve and style. Fiona forgot about her blushing partner after the first chord and danced as if she were back in the smoky hall at Strathglass. Highland dancing, well done, is more like ballet than anything else. One by one the other dancers stopped and drew to the side and watched Fiona. Poor Captain Rogers rallied amazingly. He had just been as terrified before his first battle, he remembered. He had banished the fear then by simply blocking out all thought and performing his duty. His duty now was to dance opposite Fiona Grant. He set to with a will, doing his best to emulate the graceful leaps of his partner.

The Marquess of Cleveden stood very still, head and shoulders above most of the crowd, watching Fiona Grant. Something wild and fresh and new had invaded London society, he thought, although he could not help thinking at the same time that young Captain Rogers deserved a medal for gallantry.

Fiona sank gracefully into a curtsy at the final chord. Then she returned to the present world and stood blushing and confused as London society roared its approval. But Lady Yarwood, when she had finished cheering, whispered behind her fan to Letitia Helmsdale, "I think we have all just earned three thousand pounds. Fiona was magnificent, but no gentleman will dare dance with her now. What man wants to make a cake of himself?"

This was repeated in harsher terms by the infuriated duchess when Fiona returned to her seat. And so it proved to be. Even the ungrateful captain, flushed with success, promptly signed his name *twice* in Lizzie's program and showed no sign of wanting to dance with Fiona again.

"What *will* I tell your parents?" moaned the duchess, and Fiona thought wretchedly, What shall I tell them myself when the Season is over and I have to find nine thousand pounds? She glanced around under her lashes, searching the faces of the elderly gentlemen present and wondering if the Marquess of Cleveden was among them. It was all the fault of that man with the yellow eyes, thought Fiona. He had only to appear for social disgrace to follow automatically.

The Marquess of Cleveden turned to his friend, Mr. Harry Gore and said, "I am amazed that Highland beauty is left to sit alone with only that horrible little Scotch duchess as company."

Mr. Gore, small, thin, and gossipy, shrugged expressive shoulders. "No one will dare stand up with her. Be rather like walking into the middle of the stage at the Italian opera stark naked."

"But she is so very beautiful and danced like an angel."

Mr. Gore shook his head of sparse curls. "No money. Beautiful, yes. But too wild and odd."

"The next dance is a waltz," said the marquess thoughtfully. "Miss Grant surely cannot perform the Highland fling during *that*."

"Cause a fuss if you do ask her," said Mr. Gore. "Everyone knows you don't dance with debutantes. Besides, you'll need to get permission. She ain't been to Almack's yet. That means Bellamy's got to give you permission to lead her out."

"Oh, that's easily done."

"Everyone will talk."

"My dear Harry, they always do. I have not been so entertained this age and it is a crime to see such a beauty left languishing alone."

"If you ask her to waltz, and she don't kick her heels up, you'll bring her into fashion. All the fellows try to emulate you."

"Precisely. Watch me fashionize Miss Grant!"

FOUR

Fiona sat and watched Lizzie dancing a Scottish reel in the best English manner. Lizzie did not have much animation but her shy ways appeared to appeal to her partners. Her light brown hair was elaborately curled and pomaded and her plump little figure looked neat and attractive in the expensive and deceptively simple muslin gown.

Well, here's an odd thing, thought Fiona. Lizzie, the accidental daughter, was supposed to be my chaperon and yet the duchess is treating *her* as the debutante. Amazing Lizzie! She has enormous power when it comes to worming her way into people's affections. But not mine! Am I jealous? Yes, of course I am. But there is much more to make me dislike her. There! She has just thrown me a pitying little smile. Even the duchess has deserted me. She sits over there talking to her friends and looking occasionally to make sure *Lizzie* is well and happy. And I bet that £9,000 pounds!

"Oh, dear," said Fiona out loud.

"What ails you?" demanded a voice above her head.

Fiona looked up. Lady Bellamy was standing in front of her. Behind her, looking amused, stood the man with the yellow eyes.

Fiona threw him such a scared look that the marquess was startled. He did not know that to Fiona's Highland eyes he had become a harbinger of social ruin.

"Miss Grant," Lady Bellamy went on coldly when Fiona did not answer her question, "may I present the Marquess of Cleveden who is desirous to dance the waltz with you? I have given my permission."

Damned! thought Fiona wildly. Damned, and double damned. Here was no faded gentleman past his prime who would be flattered by the attention of a young miss, but a powerful, rich, and handsome man who looked as if he could have married any woman he chose and, if the gossips were right, chose not to.

"Miss Grant!" said Lady Bellamy sharply.

Fiona pulled herself together with an effort and rose to her feet. She curtsied first to Lady Bellamy and then to the marquess. "I am honored by your invitation, my lord," she said in a hollow voice.

Lady Bellamy gave a curt little nod and walked away.

The marquess held out his hand. Avoiding his

curious gaze with all the shiftiness of Lizzie, Fiona allowed herself to be led to the floor.

She had only waltzed before with her dancing master and hoped her steps were sedate enough for this English ballroom.

When he placed his hand firmly on her waist, she experienced such a turmoil of sensation that she turned quite white.

"This will not answer, Miss Grant," said the marquess. "You look about to faint. Are you ill?"

"No, my lord," said Fiona. "I am too tight-laced." Then she colored up to the roots of her hair. What an unmaidenly excuse!

The slender waist under the marquess's hand felt soft and pliant. A flash of humor lit those odd eyes of his.

"Do you wish to retire and... er... *un*lace?"

"No, my lord," said Fiona. "I shall do very well now."

He was handsome, he was rich, but he was unmarried, and the Season stretched ahead. If only she could get him to propose, and that she would not do if she were going to turn faint at the sight of him.

She smiled up at him, a tender bewitching smile. He smiled back and swung her onto the floor among the other dancers.

There was no doubt in the minds of watching society after those first few steps that Miss Fiona Grant could waltz like an angel. There was no doubt either that Lord Cleveden was looking interested and amused.

"She has got him! She has got him!" said Letitia Helmsdale to Euphemia Perkins.

"With her looks and grace, she could get anyone," said Euphemia Perkins dismally.

"But not Cleveden," said Lady Yarwood, who had come up in time to overhear this pessimistic exchange. "Cleveden may dance with her, but he will not marry her—or anyone else. My mama says that beauty after beauty has been thrown at his head almost since he was out of short coats. Besides, why so sad? Three thousand pounds is a mere trifle as far as we are concerned."

"I will have to explain to Mama how it comes about I need such a sum," said Euphemia.

"And I," echoed Letitia.

"Oh, I regret to say I have been in this pickle before," said Lady Yarwood. "We are expected to carry card money with us, you know that. Many debutantes including myself have been caught by those hostesses who pretend they are giving card parties but are, in fact, running genteel hells. All you do is accuse Fiona Grant of being one of them and you will find your parents will pay without a murmur. One never pays one's dressmaker or jeweler until the poor things scream, but gambling debts must always be paid. Besides, although the Grants have not been long in Town, Sir Edward Grant already has the reputation of being a hardened gambler."

"I do not want to lose," said Euphemia Perkins, "and yet, on the other hand, Fiona is such an affectionate, carefree sort of girl, I find myself wanting her to win."

"Fiona is very well," agreed Lady Yarwood. "But Cleveden! Not a hope there, I can assure you."

The three fell to discussing their beaux. Lady Yarwood, the other two felt, should not be discussing other gentlemen since she was engaged to her colonel and shortly to marry him, but she did seem to have a wandering eye.

Although Fiona danced prettily, the marquess found it difficult to talk to her. Despite a feeling he was wasting his time and would soon find this enchanting-looking Highland girl was as boring as any other debutante, he suggested when the waltz finished that they should find a quiet corner and continue their conversation.

"Indeed, my lord," said Fiona with a flash of humor, "I was not aware we had even begun."

"Not at all my fault, Miss Grant," he pointed out amiably. "I made so many attempts and asked so many questions only to get yes or no by way of reply."

"After having disgraced myself by leaping about during the Sean Trews," said Fiona, "I was watching my steps too carefully to pay much attention to you."

"And, of course," teased the marquess, "there is the discomfort of tight lacing."

"I should not have said that," said Fiona. "It was not true, and in any case it was a most unladylike thing to say."

He piloted her deftly toward a sofa in a corner, half hidden from the ballroom by a potted palm.

"And so what was the reason?" he asked, waiting until she was seated and then sitting down next to her.

"I had decided you were unlucky. I saw you at the Hanover Square Concert," said Fiona, "and immediately after that was in social disgrace. I saw you enter the ballroom, and then disgraced myself again."

"You speak like a gambler. The gambler always sees signs and omens."

"Perhaps," laughed Fiona. "Are you sure I should be sitting here alone with you like this, my lord? I do not wish to endure another jaw-me-dead from the Duchess of Gordonstoun."

"Perfectly conventional," he said, quirking an eyebrow at her. "I am quite a catch."

"But not yet caught," said Fiona, amazed at her own boldness.

"No, not yet. Perhaps not ever. Tell me, I hear your parents are in Town, so why are you chaperoned by the duchess? I trust your mother is not ill."

"No, my parents were persuaded by the duchess that she herself was better suited to puffing me off."

"And yet she appears to devote her energies to your companion. A relative?"

"Yes, my lord. Lizzie Grant is a cousin."

"And this cousin, I hear, was, shortly before, a seamstress. Lady Bellamy, frightened that one of the lower orders should be soiling her ballroom floor with plebeian feet, quizzed the duchess as to the reason for Miss Lizzie Grant's presence. The duchess said Miss Grant was of good family and had merely been put to the needle to make her a better wife and housekeeper for some lucky man. A new idea! You do things very differently in Scotland."

"So it seems," said Fiona crossly. "I was under the impression that Lizzie was to be my companion. I was urged to copy her manner."

The marquess leveled his quizzing glass in the direction of Lizzie, who was, at that moment, whispering in the duchess's ear.

"Do not, I beg of you," he said finally, "copy her manner. It would not sit well with you."

"You appear very *au fait* with a great deal of trivial gossip about my family," said Fiona.

"I am *au fait* with a great deal of trivial gossip about everyone. My friend Mr. Harry Gore—the thin fussy man over there who has just tripped over his partner's feet and is now gracefully accepting *her* apologies—keeps me up to the mark."

"Gentlemen are not supposed to gossip," said Fiona.

"They have little else to do with their time," he said dryly. "Idleness breeds gossip. But I confess, I have found listening to gossip very useful in the past. It has stopped me from making quite a number of mistakes."

"With the ladies?" said Fiona sharply.

"Now, I did not say that."

"But I think that is what you meant, sir. And if that is the case, then you were wrong to listen. The ladies at the Season are very competitive. One might say wrong of another in order to disaffect you."

"Were my affections seriously engaged," he said, smiling into her eyes, "then nothing and no one could disaffect me."

Fiona found that gaze disturbing. She looked away in confusion—and found the Duchess of Gordonstoun bearing down on her with Lizzie in tow.

"My dear Cleveden," cried the duchess. "I see you have been entertaining little Fiona. May I present another Grant relative, Miss Lizzie Grant?"

The marquess rose and bowed, and then sat down again. He pointedly did not offer either Lizzie or the duchess his place on the sofa and there were no chairs nearby. The duchess realized she would be forced to take her leave, for she could not stand in front of the couple like a maid being interviewed for a job.

But she tried again. "The next dance is the quadrille," said the duchess, "and Lizzie is just pining to show her steps."

"Then may I suggest Miss Grant position herself more prominently?" said the marquess sweetly. "She will never find a partner if she hides herself in this corner."

"You are so right," said the duchess with a smile

that did not meet her eyes, eyes which looked like Scottish granite as they surveyed the marquess and Fiona. "Come, Lizzie."

The marquess thoughtfully watched them go. "Now, that, my dear Miss Grant," he said, "is very interesting. Here I am, a rich and eligible man, albeit a bit long in the tooth for a lady of your tender years, and there goes your launcher or chaperon after trying to remove me and throw me into the arms of your . . . cousin, did you say?"

"Yes," said Fiona.

"Strange, these Scottish customs. I thought Highlanders only put their by-blows to trade."

"My lord!" exclaimed Fiona, pretending to be shocked in order to silence him, for despite her dislike of the girl, Fiona knew she would never betray the secret of Lizzie's birth.

"Forgive me. I should not have said that. But if you do not wish to ruin your chances at this Season, I suggest you ask Lady Grant to chaperon you herself."

"Mama is much impressed with the duchess. And they are old friends. She will not listen to me."

"Then perhaps she will listen to me. My age will make it seem like a fatherly interest."

Fiona's heart sank. When he had smiled at her, £9,000 had seemed on the point of tumbling into her lap. Now it was whirling away.

"You are very good," she said in a dismal voice. "I think Mama will listen to me if—"

She broke off. She had been about to say "if papa has been lucky at cards."

He relapsed into silence and watched the dancers. Fiona began to wonder whether he was bored.

Then as the music finished he rose to his feet. "I must leave you to your other partners, Miss Grant. Will you walk with me tomorrow if I call for you at, say, three in the afternoon?"

"Oh, yes, my lord," said Fiona, her eyes like stars. She looked enchantedly delighted at the prospect and the marquess did not know she saw once more a chance of winning that all-important bet.

To her great surprise, no sooner had he taken his leave than she was surrounded by young men clamoring for the next dance.

The marquess watched, amused. Fiona was set to be the belle of the ball. But, he wondered, throwing a curious glance in the direction of the Duchess of Gordonstoun, what there was about Fiona's success that did not please that odd little lady.

Sir Edward and Lady Grant were asleep when Fiona arrived home. The duchess had said farewell to both Lizzie and Fiona outside, saying grimly she would call on Lady Grant on the morrow, and Fiona was sure she meant to complain about her behavior during the early part of the ball.

Miss Fiona's Fancy

She rose early next morning and waited anxiously until Christine came to say that Lady Grant was taking her morning chocolate and would be glad to see her daughter.

"Good morning, my dear," said Lady Grant, offering a plump cheek to Fiona to kiss. "I trust you enjoyed your first ball. Such news! Papa had the most tremendous luck at the tables and all debts are to be settled, including your dreadfully expensive dressmakers. Which reminds me. I was a little taken aback to receive quite a large bill for Lizzie's dresses as well. One does not want to seem uncharitable to a less fortunate member of the clan, and yet . . ."

"Oh, Mama, do but listen to me!" cried Fiona. "You must chaperon me yourself or I shall never wed." She began to tell her mother everything—about the red gown, about the marquess, and how the duchess, instead of seeming pleased and gratified by her success, tried to destroy it and put Lizzie in her place.

Lady Grant listened to her carefully. Now she was over her fear of losing the Grant estates, she could survey the situation clearly. She rang the bell and, when Christine answered, asked the maid to request Sir Edward to attend his wife.

Sir Edward came in, wrapped in an enormous silk dressing gown with a red Kilmarnock nightcap perched on top of his head.

Lady Grant made her daughter repeat her story over again, and like his wife had done, Sir Edward listened carefully. He was in a clearheaded sober mood, happy his debts were settled, determined never to gamble again.

"Cleveden!" he exclaimed. "Why, he's as rich as Golden Ball. And you say he is coming here! He must be encouraged, Fiona. He is a trifle older than I would have wished in a son-in-law, but if he proves interested in you, then we must put no obstacles in his path. Betty," he went on, meaning the duchess, "has behaved most oddly. I am sure the matter of the color of your gown was a mistake. Lizzie seems such a quiet, docile girl and she is hardly in a social position to be malicious to her betters."

Fiona experienced a stab of compassion for the unfortunate Lizzie. It was unfair to damn her socially because of her accident of birth which had been none of her fault, after all. "And you say the duchess is to call? Then I shall see her myself. No," he added, seeing his wife was about to protest. "You will be too soft with her. We will need to find out what to do about Lizzie. Perhaps I shall send her to Strathglass."

Fiona felt miserable. She did not like Lizzie. But she did not want the girl to be snatched away from all the balls and parties and pretty dresses to be sent north, no doubt to take up duties as a servant.

"Perhaps Lizzie could stay with us a little longer," she forced herself to say. "Without the duchess, she will not trouble me."

Fiona prayed the duchess would arrive before

three in the afternoon. She did not want the marquess to arrive in the middle of a squabble.

But the duchess arrived at noon. Fiona was sent out of the drawing room. She would not have known what happened had not the faithful Christine listened at the door.

The duchess had tried her best to discredit Fiona's tale of events, saying that the marquess had been merely amusing herself. The news that he was to take Fiona walking that afternoon obviously came as a shock to the duchess, for Fiona had carefully avoided mentioning the engagement. Accused by Sir Edward of having concentrated on Lizzie, the duchess hotly denounced Fiona as a sly ungrateful girl. Sir Edward went on to say that Lizzie should go north to Strathglass, where, he had no doubt, Mrs. Macleod, the housekeeper, would be glad to find some duties for her. Lizzie wept at this. The Duchess of Gordonstoun flared up and said she would take Lizzie that day under her own wing and treat the child like her own daughter. One word led to an other, and the duchess left, taking Lizzie with her and vowing to cut any of the Grants should she be unlucky enough to see any of them again.

"So Lizzie is going to be in an even better position," said Fiona. "I only hope she is really the ingenue she would have us believe."

"So all we have to do," said Christine cheerfully, "is to have you looking your best for your beau."

"I am going to have to flirt a little, Christine," said Fiona, "that is, if I hope to attract him. I do not quite know how to flirt."

"It's quite easy," said Christine. "I've watched other young ladies. You must go on as if you are very delicate and fragile. You must giggle shyly and wave your fan a lot. You must let him help you across the road. You dither on the edge as if faced with a crossing of the Tay River. On the other side, you must thank him as warmly as if he had saved you from croco-things, whatever they are."

"Crocodiles. You are quite right, Christine. I have noticed how the ladies behave. I should have thought that any man with half a brain would be bored to death with all that fluttering and giggling."

"It's what they like, miss," said Christine firmly. "Nothing disgusts a gentleman more than a strong-minded woman!"

FIVE

The Marquess of Cleveden wished he had not come. A gambler's house was often a sorry place, he thought, looking bleakly at the scarred furniture and the musty curtains. He was accustomed to avoiding people who toadied to him.

Sir Edward and his wife had certainly graceful and charming manners, but they made it quite obvious they already looked on him as a son-in-law and embarrassed him by praising his manners and dress.

Fiona herself was a disappointment, although she made a ravishing picture in a white muslin walking dress with a high ruff and with a long green stole of shot silk with a dainty green bonnet of shot silk to match.

She kept casting him arch, roguish glances.

The marquess sighed. He had been in such situations before, although not for some years now. Always there was the hope that this might be the one lady for him, and always the latest choice turned out to be as pretty and dull as all the rest.

Well, he would freeze her off with a time-tried ruse. Instead of walking, he would send for his carriage and take her on a drive through the most wretched and miserable parts of Town.

He smiled gently on Sir Edward and replied that, yes, Weston was his tailor, and yes, he got his boots from Lobb, and added, "The sky looks threatening, Sir Edward. Would you be so good as to send one of your footmen to my address and ask my servants to bring my carriage round?"

Of course, Sir Edward agreed and one of his footmen was immediately sent off.

"Now." Sir Edward beamed, refilling the marquess's glass. "We will provide you with some entertainment while we are all waiting. Do you care for the pipes?"

"I think pipe music sounds very romantic when heard from a distance of several mountains away," said the marquess.

"Ah, but the full beauty cannot be appreciated at a distance," said Sir Edward. He turned to his butler. "Dougal, ask Angus to step along."

"I really must *beg* you not to trouble," said the marquess.

"No trouble at all," said Sir Edward. "I have my own piper, Angus Robertson, and he is the best in the Highlands."

The marquess resigned himself. Angus came in with his pipes and proceeded to tune up by running up the scale. The marquess noticed that the F note sounded exactly like the squeaking of a rusty farm gate.

"What's it going to be, Angus?" Sir Edward beamed.

"'The Sassenach's Awa'," said Angus maliciously, the title meaning, "The Englishman Has Gone."

"No, I don't think..." began Sir Edward, but with a ferocious skirl, Angus began to play.

Was there ever such a noise? The marquess sat, stunned and deafened as the wail of the pipes like ten thousand cats in the agonies of death bounced off the walls.

He looked at Fiona. She sat with a dreamy smile on her face, her foot tapping.

I have wandered among savages, thought the marquess bleakly.

At last the horrible noise wailed off into silence.

"What have you to say to *that*, my lord?" said Sir Edward, rubbing his hands.

"I am beyond words," said the marquess faintly.

"Aye, 'tis a grand sound. Play his lordship something else."

"My carriage!" cried the marquess in relief. "Sir Edward, I shall return your daughter to you shortly. Lady Grant, your servant."

He led Fiona from the room.

"Clever Fiona," said Sir Edward with an indulgent smile. "I like a man who enjoys the pipes. You did fine, Angus."

"Never do anything else," said Angus Robertson laconically.

Fiona, remembering Christine's advice, dithered and squeaked as she was handed up into his lordship's high-perched phaeton. What a long way from the ground it was, she exclaimed. Quite terrifying!

The marquess said nothing and set his team in motion.

Fiona set herself to please. She exclaimed over the fine buildings and churches. She exclaimed at the beauty of the trees in the Park, she commented roguishly on the beauty of the London ladies.

The marquess answered her politely while driving steadily away from the fashionable West End. Soon, he guessed, she would fall silent, then she would try to tease him about their miserable surroundings, and then she would beg to be taken home.

As they began to move down mean streets under the shadow of crumbling buildings, Fiona raised a scented handkerchief to her nose. The smell was sickening and the condition of the children in the streets, heartbreaking. She had seen scenes of poverty before, particularly on her road south, but there was something so hideous about so many poor people being crammed together in these reeking sunless streets where the tottering buildings almost met overhead.

The marquess noticed Fiona had fallen silent. She sat bolt upright beside him, her eyes wide. Any moment now, she would tell him to turn about.

"Stop!" cried Fiona suddenly.

"Why?" he asked innocently.

Her answer surprised him. "Down that street—there!" said Fiona. "There is a man beating a child while everyone looks on."

"They send the children out in gangs to thieve handkerchiefs and things like that," he said. "If they return empty-handed, they are beaten."

Before he could even guess what she meant to do, she had seized his whip out of his hand and leapt down nimbly from the high perch.

"Miss Grant!" he called, appalled.

But she was running straight down the street toward the man beating the little girl.

The marquess looked around. "Here, you!" he called to a thickset man who was staring openmouthed at the elegant carriage. "A guinea if you hold these horses and beat off anyone who tries to annoy them."

"Right, guv," said the man cheerfully. "For a guinea, I'd fight Mendoza 'isself.'" Mendoza, the Israelite, was the latest hero of the ring.

The marquess sprinted down the street after Fiona. She was in the process of laying about the man's shoulders with the whip while the crowd stood looking on in amazement.

He wrenched the whip from Fiona's hands, and said, "Come along, Miss Grant. There is nothing you can do here."

"Oh, yes I can," said Fiona. She put an arm about the sobbing girl. "What is your name?"

"Polly," sobbed the dirty scrap of humanity.

"How old are you?"

"Fifteen year, they say," whined the girl. Fiona realized the girl was so small and wizened that she could easily have mistaken her for a small child.

"Then you shall come with me and wear clean clothes and . . . and . . . have food and learn a trade."

Polly dried her eyes on her skirt. "You mean you'll take me away from him?" she said, pointing a grubby finger at her tormentor.

"Yes."

"Right," said Polly with a grin, as happy now as she had been wretched a moment before.

"For heaven's saske, Miss Grant," said the marquess. "Get a move on. Things are about to turn ugly."

An evil-looking group of men and women were pressing closer, staring greedily at the marquess and Fiona's rich clothes.

"Start walking quickly toward the carriage," said the marquess, "but do not run and do not show any sign of fear."

"I am not afraid," said Fiona coldly. "Come, Polly."

She took the girl by the hand and began to lead her down the street to the carriage. "Get Jenkins," called a shrill female voice. "Jenkins'll do fer 'im."

" 'Ere comes Jenkins," called another voice. And then another said, "Mr. Jenkins, this 'ere swell's taking away Reilly's girl."

"I'll see to 'im," said a deep voice. The marquess groaned inwardly and turned about. A mountain of a man was pushing his way to the front of the crowd.

Cursing Fiona under his breath, the marquess raised his fists.

Fiona settled Polly in the carriage. The high perch afforded her a grandstand view of the fight. She was just debating with herself whether to try to handle the ribbons herself and drive in search of a parish constable, prompted by Polly's sad little remark of, "Mr. Jenkins will kill your fellow, missus. 'E allus kills people," when the man mountain that was Jenkins seemed to fly through the air to land with a great crash.

There was an enormous cheer from the onlookers, now as friendly to the marquess as they had been hostile before. They huzzaed and cheered him all the way to the phaeton.

The marquess tossed a guinea to the man who was guarding the horses and climbed in. His cravat was torn and his lip was split and bleeding.

"I *am* sorry," said Fiona as they drove off. "Are you most dreadfully hurt?"

"No, Miss Grant. I shall live."

"Well," went on Fiona in a small voice, "it *was* a very odd place to take me for a drive."

"I lost my way," lied the marquess grimly. "Are you really going to take that child into your home?"

"Of course," said Fiona, wide-eyed. "She has nowhere else to go except back to that horrible man. Have you, Polly?"

"No, mum," said Polly cheerfully. "I be ever so grateful, mum. Pinch all the wipes you want."

"She means," explained the marquess, "that she will steal all the handkerchiefs you desire."

"Oh, you must not steal anymore, Polly," said Fiona. "Stealing is wrong."

"Right," said Polly, folding her skinny arms across her chest and gazing about her in delight.

The marquess felt obliged to say when they returned to the Grant home facing Hyde Park, "Do you wish me to come indoors, Miss Grant? I fear your parents will be alarmed and might not welcome this addition to their household."

"Oh, no," said Fiona. "They are very understanding." Summoning up her courage, she added, "I hope to see you again, soon, my lord."

All his old disappointment in her returned. She was simpering at him and batting her eyelashes.

"I am afraid I shall be very busy over the next few weeks, Miss Grant," he said.

Fiona looked very cast down and seemed about to cry. But he decided he had already wasted too much time with her. He merely smiled and inclined his head, waiting until he had led the disgraceful Polly inside and shut the door.

Sir Edward and Lady Grant accepted Polly's arrival without much fuss. They were used to clansmen and odd relatives popping up on the doorstep. Polly was sent below to the kitchens to begin her training as a maid.

But Fiona's parents were distressed when Fiona described her drive.

Miss Fiona's Fancy

"Oh, you must not have anything more to do with him," cried Lady Grant. "Such a disappointment. Imagine taking a young lady to the slums for a drive!"

"I *was* puzzled," said Fiona. "It's not as if he is a reformer or a preacher or anyone who plans to alleviate the conditions there. Perhaps he is one of those peculiar people who enjoy other people's misery."

"You made that up," pointed out Sir Edward. "No one enjoys another human being's misery."

"Then why do thousands of people turn up to see a public hanging?" snapped Fiona. "I bet the Marquess of Clevedon reserves a front seat."

"You do?" said her father. "How much?"

"Edward!" cautioned his wife. "You promised!"

"Oh, yes," mumbled Sir Edward, "so I did."

Fiona went up to her room and regaled Christine with the whole story.

"How very odd!" exclaimed the maid. "Well, there's fine men aplenty in London. No need to bother your pretty head with an eccentric."

"But I must," wailed Fiona, thinking of her bet. She was mad ever to have made it. And now the family fortunes had been saved without her doing one thing about it!

"Why?" asked Christine. "Never say you are spoony about him."

"Of course not."

"Then what?"

"He is rich, and I must marry well."

"But there are others. Do be sensible, Miss Fiona, dear. Everything is going so nicely. That Lizzie Grant sent for her traps. You are supposed to be enjoying yourself as well, miss. What if you don't find a man to suit? There is always Mr. Jamie."

"Oh yes," said Fiona gloomily, thinking of Jamie Grant. "There's always Jamie."

The Marquess of Cleveden sat at the desk in his library and worked on an impassioned speech he hoped to deliver to the House of Lords concerning the miserable condition of children among London's poor. Did Fiona realize just how many children and girls like Polly there were thieving for a living? And what would she say, or what would any other girl say, when they found out about his slum charities?"

Probably think he was mad, thought the marquess, throwing good money away to help a lot of paupers. His fortune, he cynically believed, was what drew the ladies to him. They would expect that fortune to be spent on gowns and baubles and would no doubt scream in horror at the size of the sums he gave away to his orphanages and charities.

His lip throbbed and he stood up and went to the mirror over the fireplace and studied it. The swelling seemed to be going down a little. Damn Fiona Grant. While she was defending that Polly, she had been magnificent, the sort of woman he had dreamed of. But then she had simpered and ogled him as she had left in a most vulgar way.

His butler, Osborne, entered, not a shaggy Highlander like the Grants' butler, but a smooth, fat, pompous man.

"There is a female person here to see you, my lord," said Osborne.

"Really, Osborne! I trust you sent her packing!"

"No, my lord. She is in great distress and appears to be a lady."

"Then why did you say *person* in the first place?"

"Because she is not accompanied by a maid, my lord, and is heavily veiled."

"And does this person give a name?"

"Miss Grant, my lord."

The marquess's thin black brows snapped together. Then he said, "Give me a few moments, Osborne. If I do not send for you again, show her in."

When the butler had gone, the marquess wondered whether to send for Osborne again and tell him to show Miss Fiona Grant out into the street. Or should he give her a dressing down? He thought wearily of all the debutantes who had dreamed up every trick to bring themselves to his notice. But not one of them had ever been so bold or so heedless of her reputation as to call at his town house.

He stayed where he was. At last the door opened and Osborne ushered in a small, plump, heavily veiled figure.

The marquess's eyes narrowed. Unless Fiona

Grant was a witch and had contrived to shrink in height, then this was certainly not she.

He nodded to Osborne who bowed and withdrew.

"You are not the Miss Grant I know," said the marquess curtly. "Who are you?"

She raised her hands and put back her veil, revealing the timid features of Lizzie Grant.

"I would not have done such an unconventional thing," she whispered, "but I felt you had to know the truth about Fiona."

"Why should the truth, or lies, about Miss Grant concern me?"

"All society knows you showed an unusual interest in her at the Bellamy's ball."

"You are impertinent, miss."

Lizzie began to sob in a dreary snuffling way. "I-I sh-should n-not have come," she choked.

"Sit down and unburden yourself, girl, if it makes you feel any better. What is this terrible thing about Fiona Grant that I should know?"

"She is going to marry you."

The marquess visibly relaxed.

" 'Odso! She will need to be asked first. Or does she plan to drag me to the altar?"

"She *must* marry you."

"Must?"

"She has made the most awful bet. She bet Miss Perkins, Miss Helmsdale, and Lady Yarwood three thousand pounds each that you would propose to her before the Season was over."

"What a gossipy lot we are, to be sure," said the

marquess evenly. " 'Twill make a vastly entertaining story, particularly when it gets about that you came, unattended, to my home to spike your cousin's guns."

Lizzie turned paper white. "No!" she gasped. "You must not tell anyone it was I. I only told you because it was my duty . . ."

"Yes," said the marquess, "you *are* stupid, are you not? Society would merely laugh at Fiona Grant, but they might consider Miss Lizzie Grant to be dangerous and spiteful."

"I only did it for the best," wailed Lizzie.

"Then if you do not wish me to betray you, I suggest you never interfere in Fiona Grant's life again or I shall most certainly tell society about it. Good day to you!"

Lizzie turned to go. Then she half turned back, lowered her veil over her face, and said in a hard little voice, "You are called Miss Fiona's Fancy. In the bet, you know. They made a betting book."

He made no reply, and so she left.

The marquess sat down at his desk again. So that was why Fiona was flirting and ogling so desperately. The minx.

He leaned back in his chair and began to laugh. He could hardly wait to see Miss Fiona again!

SIX

The Prince Regent adored anything and everything Scottish, mainly thanks to the works of Walter Scott and the Prince's own romantic disposition.

Fiona's wild Highland dance had not, therefore, damned her in the eyes of society, nor had the withdrawal of the Duchess of Gordonstoun's help. The duchess was not popular, and now she had turned her back on her only friend, the easygoing Lady Grant, she was left with Lizzie for company.

The fact that she doted on the girl was evident. She chaperoned her as zealously as any matchmaking mama and sternly quelled any rumors about Lizzie's doubtful birth. For society still speculated as to why any gently born miss should have been sent to a dressmaker for an apprenticeship.

Fiona felt embarrassed at meeting Lizzie at balls and parties—for although the duchess was disliked, she was also feared because of her hectoring, bullying manner, and most hostesses were not brave enough to close their doors to her or Lizzie. But after a week of seeing Lizzie everywhere, she and the duchess disappeared. Christine, the maid, who was very good at picking up snippets of gossip, reported the duchess had taken Lizzie to Bath, considering the society of that famous spa "more genteel" than London.

Relieved not to have to face the contemptuous, angry duchess or see Lizzie's sly sidelong looks, Fiona set out to win the heart of the Marquess of Cleveden with renewed zeal. He had been present during that week at a few of the parties and functions, but although he had smiled and nodded to her, he had not approached her. Fiona wondered what to do next.

She did not know the marquess was gleefully waiting to see just what she *would* do.

Lady Grant was puzzled by her daughter's behavior. Several very attractive and eligible young men had started to call and send poems and bouquets of flowers, but Fiona seemed uninterested in them all.

As ten whole days since Fiona had last spoken to the marquess went past she began to feel desperate. In order to clear her thoughts, she went riding in the Row early one morning with Angus, the piper. They were trotting along under the trees when Fiona suddenly saw the marquess cantering toward them on a tall black Arabian horse. He raised his hat to Fiona, nodded and smiled, and rode on.

"Stop!" cried Fiona to Angus. "Did you see that man who passed us?"

"I did not mark him," said Angus laconically. "I was thinking of something else."

"He sneered at me," said Fiona.

"Oh, he did, did he?" said Angus. "Well, we'll see about that!"

He wheeled his horse about and spurred it after the marquess.

Now what have I done? thought Fiona wildly. But I had to do something.

She followed the piper.

Angus had come alongside the marquess. Both men had reined in their mounts. Angus was shouting something, and the marquess was looking angry and amazed.

Fiona rode up to them just as Angus was saying, "Get down from that horse and let's see what you're made of."

"Angus, what *is* the matter?" said Fiona, all innocence.

"This man sneered at you, you said," replied Angus.

"Oh, Angus, I only said he *smiled* at me. This is the Marquess of Cleveden."

"Miss Fiona, you said—"

"Do forgive Angus," said Fiona, dimpling up at the marquess, who surveyed her with a hard cynical gaze. "He has become a trifle deaf."

But Angus was no London servant to stand by and listen while his mistress told blatant lies about him. "Wait till I tell Sir Edward," said Angus. "Me! Angus Robertson! The finest and sharpest ear in the glens to be so insulted. If your ruse was to force the gentleman to speak to you, you should have said so." And then turning to the marquess, "Pray accept my deepest apologies, my lord." He rode a little away, leaving the marquess alone with Fiona.

Fiona felt thoroughly ashamed of herself. It would have been bad enough to have lied to an ordinary servant, but to lie to her father's piper was ten times' worse. A piper held a special place in the household and was treated with courtesy and respect by his master. She forced herself to meet the marquess's gaze. "It was a misunderstanding," she faltered.

He smiled. "How churlish of me not to grasp at any excuse to talk to you. You are looking very beautiful today, Miss Grant."

"Thank you," she said curtly, and then, to his amusement, she rallied and fluttered her eyelashes. "I do not think my beauty could ever match the beauty of your compliments," she said.

How far, he wondered, was Miss Fiona prepared to go in her pursuit of him?

"Have you been enjoying your first Season?" he asked.

"Not much," said Fiona. "I mean," she added hurriedly, "I have not been about much yet, but 'tis vastly amusing."

"I confess to being a trifle bored," he replied. "But perhaps tonight's entertainment will be different."

"What do you attend this evening?"

"A masked ball at the Pantheon. May I hope to see you there? I would like the pleasure of waltzing with you again."

"But . . . but the Pantheon is no longer respectable."

"Ah, Miss Grant, you do not know how much I long to meet a lady who would do something, just once, that is *not* considered respectable."

"London abounds in the Fashionable Impure," said Fiona tartly. "I am sure any of *them* would be delighted to oblige you."

"Tut, tut, Miss Grant. I was thinking of the lady of my dreams, the lady I mean to marry."

"I was only funning," said Fiona hurriedly. "Of course I shall be there."

"May I escort you?"

"N-no, my lord. I shall see you there. I hope you recognize me."

"I shall recognize you, Miss Grant, even when you are masked. I look forward to seeing you."

He bowed and rode off.

Now what am I to do? thought Fiona. Mama does not approve of Cleveden because he took me driving in the slums. She would certainly not allow me to go to the Pantheon, even if the Prince Regent himself were to invite me. But I must go.

Angus rode up to her, scowling. Fiona said, "Are you going to report me to Papa, Angus?"

"Aye, save you do one thing for me."

"And what is that?"

"Contrive a way to get me into the company of Christine Grant."

"Christine! But you see her every day, Angus."

"She never has any free time. She's always on duty, and in the servants' hall, she does not sit near me."

"I'll think of something, Angus," promised Fiona. "Only don't tell Papa!"

When she got home, Fiona poured out her troubles to Christine, ending up with the added complication of Angus's desire to have some time with the maid. To her surprise, Christine blushed rosily and looked pleased and gratified.

"Don't you see," cried Christine, "we can now solve all problems! Lady Grant has been complaining of fatigue and wishes a quiet evening at home. Sir Edward, I am afraid, wishes to go to his club this evening."

"Oh, dear," said Fiona. "I think he promised Mama he would not gamble."

"When did a gambler ever keep his promise?" said Christine. "But only listen, Miss Fiona. We will all go masked to the Pantheon—that is, you, me, and Angus. Angus and I will be there to protect you because I have heard these affairs can be somewhat scandalous. Also, I do not trust this marquess. Why are you so desperate to do what he wants?"

MISS FIONA'S FANCY

"I may as well tell you, Christine," said Fiona, "but you must not talk to anyone, even Angus."

"I promise. Go on."

So Fiona told her about the bet. "You see, Christine," she ended, "Papa no longer needs the money, so I only have to get him to propose and then I shall have enough money to be truly independent."

"I fear you are as hardened a gambler as your father," said Christine. "Women are never independent. Besides, I have heard talk of this marquess. He does not appear to be in the least interested in getting married. He is much older than you. I fear you will find he is having fun at your expense. Why not appeal to the three ladies with whom you made the bet? Tell them it was a joke."

"Oh, I could never do that!" said Fiona, shocked. "A wager is a wager."

"Very well. If we must go, we must go. I will sew masks for the three of us. Then this evening I shall tell Lady Grant you have the headache and I have given you something to make you sleep. I shall say I am not feeling well either. She is a kind mistress and will let me retire for the evening, particularly as she is not going out."

"Do we work you very hard, Christine?" asked Fiona. "Angus said you never have any free time."

"I like being busy," said Christine comfortably. "I never thought to ask for free time, but," she added with a twinkle in her eye, "that was before I knew Angus was interested in me."

* * *

Fiona and Christine made silent and hurried preparations for the masquerade. The large shabby house near Hyde Park corner had a little-used staircase that led out into the garden. They planned to leave by that way and then out of the garden and into the street where they would hail a hack.

Excited by the forthcoming adventure, Fiona spent a long time deciding what to wear and then at last settled on a white muslin gown with an overdress of gold gauze. Christine had fashioned a mask for Fiona out of gold velvet and had edged it with little gold beads. Fiona pressed the maid to borrow one of her dresses, but Christine said it would be better if she continued to look like Fiona's maid so that the marquess would know Miss Grant had servants with her to protect her. In finer clothes, said Christine, the marquess might take her for a rakish friend. No respectable lady went to the Pantheon, said Christine, and surely this lord was a bad man to even suggest such a thing.

But Fiona was too anxious to win that bet to start worrying about the Marquess of Cleveden's morals. "I only want him to propose to me, Christine," she protested. "I am not going to *marry* him."

Fiona was unable to have a bath. The water supply from the Thames, and New River, was only turned on three times a week to the houses of London and that evening did not fall on one of the three days. She contented herself with scrubbing herself down while standing in a bowl of water, which is all the kitchen would allow her from the precious supply they saved on "off" days for the more important things like cooking and brewing tea.

Angus was waiting for them in the garden when they slipped out of the house, a fine cravat tied round his neck and the gleam of a gold-embroidered waistcoat Fiona recognized as one of her father's under his cloak. Angus, at any rate, had no intention of looking like a servant.

The normally languid piper seemed strung-up and talkative by the mere sight of Christine. How old was Angus? wondered Fiona. He must be nearly forty. And Christine was her own age, and yet Christine obviously did not consider the piper old.

They walked in silence to Hyde Park corner where Angus hailed a hack. Once inside the smelly carriage, they donned their masks.

Christine and Angus disappeared to be replaced by two sinister-looking strangers. They do not look like the people I know, thought Fiona. If I had said I would meet *them* at the ball, then I never would have recognized them. What if Cleveden does not recognize me?

The press of carriages in Oxford Street was so great that they stopped the hack and got out to walk the short distance to the pillared portico of the Pantheon. Fiona had received some pin money from her father when he was in a generous mood after his last win. It was enough to pay the hack and pay their entrance fee of half a crown each, and yet leave enough to pay for refreshments when they got inside.

They made their way to a box overlooking the floor. There were a great many people, all looking very fashionable. Fiona began to relax. It was all quite respectable. But a second look showed her that the ladies wore remarkably little even for this age of scanty fashions. The third look told her they were not ladies. There was a certain glittering boldness about the eyes behind the masks, a certain flaunting of bodies as they turned and twisted in the dance. No one was as yet openly misbehaving but Fiona was suddenly sure they would, before the night was out.

And where was Cleveden? And how would he ever find her? The boxes were rapidly filling up with noisy groups of people. The dance floor was becoming more and more crowded.

Angus Robertson closely questioned a tired and contemptuous waiter as to the cheapest thing they could order and settled for a bowl of punch.

Fiona felt better after a few glasses of punch, not knowing quite how powerful the mixture was.

Angus and Christine were sitting a little behind her, talking in low voices. Fiona wanted to ask them to sit beside her in the box so that she did not feel so exposed, but they were obviously so wrapped up in each other that she did not like to nip this obviously growing romance in the bud.

Then Angus leaned forward and asked her permission to take Christine down to the floor for a dance. Fiona hesitated, not wanting to be left alone. But no one had pestered her or showed any intention of doing so. She agreed and watched Christine and Angus make their way down one of the many staircases from the ranks of boxes to the floor.

Then she was besieged by men—men with glittering eyes behind their masks and loose mouths. Men who grew sulky and rude when she refused to dance.

Suddenly one man, bolder than the rest, returned to the box, seized her roughly round the waist, and tried to drag her to her feet.

"It's no use playing Miss Prunes and Prisms with me," he growled. "Ladies don't come here."

Fiona slapped his masked face. "You'll give me a kiss for that, you jade," he said, returning to the attack. He was large and fat and sweating. He smelled abominably. Fiona cried for help but the people in the other boxes only looked highly amused and cheered her tormentor on to further efforts.

And then a hand seized his collar and swung him around. Tall, furious, yellow eyes blazing, the Marquess of Cleveden said, "Be on your way, fellow, before I throw you out of this box onto the floor."

Fiona's attacker was large, but he took one scared look at the marquess's grim mouth and those terrible blazing eyes glowing behind a black mask, mumbled an apology, and escaped as fast as he could.

"I am sorry I was delayed," said the marquess, sitting down beside Fiona, who was vigorously fanning herself and forcing herself not to scream at him for having been instrumental in getting her to come to such a place.

The sitting at the House of Lords had gone on longer than the marquess had expected. He had rushed home and scrambled into his evening dress, wondering what had possessed him to think up such a mad escapade.

He had finally and successfully given Fiona Grant a disgust of him, of that he was sure. Bet or no bet, he was sure she would never want to see him again.

And then he noticed her eyes were shining with tears.

"I am a monster," he said. "How could I have done such a thing to you? But you were a widgeon to come."

"Then why did you ask me?"

"To see how far you were prepared to go."

"I do not understand you, my lord."

"To see how far you were prepared to go in your pursuit of me."

"My lord!"

"Dry your tears and listen to me, Fiona Grant. Will you tell me why you normally flirt and simper in that quite dreadful way when you see me? I judge you to be a tolerably strong-minded woman, not given to being missish."

Fiona took out a wisp of handkerchief and dabbed at her eyes. Then she sat with her head bowed, feeling this was the time to say something to charm him, but unable to think of anything.

The marquess watched her carefully. So she would not trust him! But that was understandable. If you wish to marry a man, you don't tell him it is only because you want to win a bet.

He continued to study her thoughtfully, and as he looked at her, the noise and chatter of the Pantheon died away. He had a strange feeling of enchantment, a mixture of tenderness and humor. Fiona Grant would never bore him. She might lie to him, infuriate him, and drag him into incredible situations, but he was sure, although he barely knew her, that she would never be tedious.

The Marquess of Cleveden leaned back in his chair and crossed his long legs. He was about to gamble seriously for the first time in his life. If he made a mistake, then it would be a mistake he would have to live with for the rest of his life. But if his instinct proved right, he might even have a glimpse of heaven.

"Miss Fiona Grant," said the Marquess of Cleveden, "will you marry me?"

SEVEN

Of course Fiona did not believe him. He was making fun of her. She looked about wildly for some sign of Angus and Christine. Where were they?

She did not know that they had been fighting their way through the dancers to rescue her when they saw the arrival of the Marquess of Cleveden and witnessed him dealing with Fiona's persecutor. Still, Christine would have pressed on, for she did not trust the marquess, but all the pushing and shoving had thrown her against Angus's chest. He held her tightly and said, "I do love you, Christine," and Christine promptly forgot about anything and everyone but the piper.

"You have not answered my question, Miss Grant," prompted the marquess.

Fiona took a deep breath. She knew what she must do to end this ridiculous business. She must confess to her father, tell him of the bet, and then never have anything to do with this mocking, tormenting, dangerous marquess again. And having come to that decision, she felt quite light-headed with relief. She could be herself. No longer must she masquerade as a simpering miss.

"I never answer stupid questions," said Fiona. "I should never have come here. As soon as Angus and Christine return, I shall take my leave."

"So you did not come unaccompanied. Wise girl. But I do not jest. I want to marry you."

"Why?" asked Fiona bluntly.

"You amuse me, Miss Grant."

"At least you are not swearing to undying love."

"No. But then I hardly know you."

"Amusement is not grounds enough for marriage."

"In my case, it is."

Fiona studied those odd eyes of his. "Are you *really* asking me to marry you?"

"Yes, Miss Grant, I *really* am."

Fiona felt a rush of heady elation. He meant it! She had made a fantastic bet. And she had won! All she had to do was to make sure he announced the engagement, collect the money, and then cry off. It was not as if he were in love with her. Only amused. He would soon find some other lady to amuse him. Besides, a gentleman who played tricks like taking her for a drive in the worst part of London—for she had not believed his excuse—and then encouraging her to attend this affair surely deserved to have the tables turned on him.

"Then, my lord," she said, "I accept your offer."
"Why?"
Fiona began to feel irritated. "What if I said I loved you?" she remarked.
"Then I should not believe you."
"I have no dowry to speak of."
"That I do believe. But we are not at the moment discussing why I wish to marry *you*, I am waiting to hear why you have accepted my proposal."

Somehow, Fiona at last sensed that a conventional fluttering of the eyelashes and a slap on the wrist with a fan would not answer. She looked at him steadily and said, "Because it amuses me to do so."

"And that is the only reason?"

No, thought Fiona, I stand to win £9,000. She looked away from him, wondering how to avoid telling him a direct lie. She had lied to him about Angus that day in the Park and it had been a nasty feeling. She became aware of the gross antics and some of the dancers. Her face flamed under her mask, and she said, "Oh, where is Angus? And Christine? I should never have come."

"And I should never have suggested such a thing," he said ruefully. "Come. Let me take you out of here."

"But my servants!"

"They are perfectly capable of finding their own way home."

At that moment, Angus and Christine came back into the box.

"You are just in time to say good night to your mistress," said the marquess.

"Aye," said Angus, "it is no place for a respectable female."

"But you may congratulate me," said the marquess. "Miss Grant has promised to marry me."

Christine let out a sharp exclamation and Fiona threw her a warning look. 'Odso, thought the marquess. So the maid knows of the bet.

Angus and Christine then offered their congratulations and said they could find their own way back to the Grant mansion.

Fiona hesitated outside the Pantheon. "Perhaps it would be better, my lord, if I took a hack. That is how I came. Mama believes I am in bed."

"How did you leave home?"

"By a little gate in the garden."

"Then I will take you near your home and you may return the way you came. I shall call on your father tomorrow."

When his carriage arrived, Fiona saw with relief it was an open one. She was shy at the thought of being closeted with him in a closed carriage. He had a tiger standing on the backstrap, so they were chaperoned in a way.

The marquess tucked a rug about her and took off his mask before he picked up the reins. Fiona took off her own mask and tucked it in her reticule.

"You have not asked me," said the marquess, sounding amused, "when we are to be married."

"I assumed sometime next year perhaps," said Fiona cautiously.

"On the contrary, I assumed sometime before the end of the month."

Fiona's hands began to shake and she tucked them under the rug. It did not matter, she reminded herself sternly. She would drop him as soon as the three girls paid up their bets.

"It is all very quick," she said. "No one surely gets married *that* quickly."

"It is easy to produce a special license. Can you think of any reason why we should wait, we who find each other so frightfully amusing?"

"No, my lord," said Fiona, wondering whether to tell her father after all or whether to simply disappear somewhere and live out the rest of her years a spinster.

"Good. I like the idea of a quiet wedding. Does that appeal to you, my love?"

"Yes," said Fiona bleakly. She stole a glance at him. His profile looked very strong, very masculine. But surely a man who proposed on a whim would accept a termination of the engagement just as lightly?

She sat in silence, gnawing her bottom lip and worrying.

At last she cried, "Stop! I shall get down here. Do not drive right up to the door."

He reined in his horses, called to his tiger to go to their heads, and then jumped down and went round to her side of the carriage. He held up his arms to help her down from the high perch.

She jumped lightly down and he held her tightly against him.

He put one hand at the nape of her neck. His lips began to descend.

"Your servant," whispered Fiona.

"He may consider himself privileged to witness the first kiss between the most amusing people in London. Dear me, Fiona, never say you do not *like* me!"

"It is not that, my lord. I have never been kissed before. I am shy."

"Shut your eyes," he teased. " 'Twill all be over in a trice—like getting a tooth pulled."

Fiona screwed her eyes shut. His mouth came down on her own, warm and pleasant and firm. Nothing to be afraid of, she thought with relief, not realizing the marquess was deliberately giving her nothing to be afraid of.

When he raised his lips, she drew away. "Good night," she said breathlessly. "I must go. I really must go."

"Till tomorrow," he said. He raised his hand in salute and sprang back into his carriage.

Fiona let herself in by the garden gate. The marquess sat and watched her until she disappeared into the blackness of the trees.

"Now, how will Sir Edward receive my proposal," he said to himself. "Rumor has it he has been winning recently so he will probably be high and mighty. Fiona will collect her winnings and then send me to the rightabout. I am sure I could make her love me, given a little time. Ah, well, it will be interesting to see what excuse she finds to break the engagement!"

When the Marquess of Cleveden called next day, Sir Edward Grant was in two minds whether to receive him or not. His wife was out shopping and Fiona was in her room. He at first wondered whether he owed the marquess any money, but he was sure he had settled all debts, and although the people he had gambled with during long drunken evenings were often hard to remember, he was sure the Marquess of Cleveden had not been one of them.

He told Dougal, the butler, to show the marquess in.

The marquess was interested to notice the change in Sir Edward's manner. Here was no Scottish landowner on the edge of ruin fawning over him, but a rather testy, grim-faced man who curtly asked him why he had called.

"I wish to marry your daughter, Fiona," said the marquess.

Sir Edward rang the bell. "Dougal," he said, when his butler reappeared, "I think we'll have some whisky if there is any left in that barrel we brought down from the north."

"You shouldnae touch the stuff," said Dougal. "Claret's better for your head."

I hope Fiona doesn't thrust a household of Highland servants on me, thought the marquess. They always answer back.

"Get it, man," said Sir Edward. "That is, if you haven't drunk the lot yourself."

Dougal growled something in Gaelic. Sir Edward growled back in the same language and the butler left to return some moments later with a decanter and two glasses. The marquess looked suspiciously at the clear liquid and then cautiously took a sip. It scorched its way down his throat to make, he felt, a large hole in his stomach.

Sir Edward drank his own glassful in one gulp and then poured himself another one. Then he turned bright curious eyes on the marquess.

"Why on earth do you want to marry Fiona?" he asked.

"Why does any man usually want to marry a lady?" countered the marquess.

"This being London," said Sir Edward dryly, "I should say, most of the time, for money."

"Not in this case."

Sir Edward thought hard. He could not be sure his phenomenal run of luck would last. Cleveden was rich, very rich. And titled. Quite a catch. But now that the panic about debts had gone, he was once more concerned for the happiness of his daughter.

"May I ask your age, sir?" he demanded.

"I am thirty-seven years of age."

"Fiona is nineteen. She is young. You are middle-aged."

"Sadly, yes. I trust that the great difference in our ages will not prevent your daughter from accepting my offer. Come, sir. I am prepared to be generous in the matter of the marriage settlements."

Sir Edward's eyes gleamed, but then he shook his head. "I cannot press my daughter to marry anyone she does not want."

"Then why do you not send for her and ask her yourself?"

Sir Edward sent for Fiona, and while the two men waited for her, he surveyed his visitor while he made general conversation. The marquess, he reflected, looked a hard-faced sophisticate. He was handsome and well built. His thick black hair had no trace of gray. But his aura of mastery combined with the almost terrifying elegance of his dress made him, to Sir Edward's eyes, a foreign creature, unsuited to be the husband of a Highland girl.

Fiona came into the room. She was wearing a morning gown of gray silk with a high white crepe ruff. It had white crepe sleeves and a belt ornamented with a clasp of jet and she wore a long necklace of Whitby jet, purchased on the journey south.

Her lashes were very long and dark, the marquess noticed, and once more he was fascinated by those little red lights like sparks that glinted among the thick tresses of her hair. He remembered the fresh, young feel of her lips against his own and his heartbeats quickened. Up till that moment, he had resigned himself to going along with that ridiculous bet—even prepared to take Fiona's breaking of the engagement. But now, he realized, he would do anything to keep her. Well, almost anything, he thought cynically. Driving Sir Edward back to the gambling tables and into debt again he could not do, although it would be a certain way of ensuring his support.

"Fiona," began Sir Edward, "the Marquess of Cleveden has asked my permission to pay his addresses to you."

"Yes, Papa," said Fiona meekly.

"He wants to marry you," went on Sir Edward, thinking she had not quite understood.

"Yes, Papa."

"You mean you accept him?"

"Yes, Papa."

"Well, I'm d— Never mine, here is your mother. Annie, Cleveden here wants to marry Fiona and she's accepted."

"Oh, my silly child," said Lady Grant, "there is no need to do that. We are not in debt."

Goodness, thought the marquess, I am going to have some very plain-speaking in-laws.

"I know we are not in debt," said Fiona. "I have, nonetheless, agreed to marry Cleveden."

The marquess listened, highly entertained, as his beloved proceeded to try to convince her parents that she actually wanted to marry a man who had been for years regarded as one of the biggest catches on the marriage mart.

"We are getting married in two weeks' time," added the marquess gently when Fiona had finished speaking. "We have no reason to wait."

"And no reason to rush either, I hope?" snapped Sir Edward.

"No, no," said the marquess soothingly.

"When did you discuss all this with Fiona?" asked Sir Edward. "When you were touring the slums?"

"We have met since then," pointed out the marquess.

"That is true, my dear," added Lady Grant, quite forgetting that the marquess had not addressed a word to her daughter at any of the social gatherings they had attended.

"Then we shall leave you alone with Fiona for a little," said Sir Edward. "We shall discuss the question of the marriage settlements later."

The marquess and Fiona faced each other when her parents had left the room.

"Well, my love," he said. "if you do not know what to do now, I shall tell you. I say, 'Alone at last.' You blush shyly. I take you in my arms and you tremble with rapture."

"Nonsense."

"You are going to have to tremble with rapture sometime or another, my sweeting. We *are* to be married."

"Can't we leave all that . . .er . . . side of things until after the wedding?" said Fiona.

"As you like. But I would not mind a kiss just now."

"Very well," said Fiona, pursing her lips and closing her eyes.

Nothing happened.

Her eyes flew open.

"No," he teased. "No more kisses, Fiona Grant, until you at least look as if you want one."

He bowed to her and left.

Fiona had to endure an hour of questions from both her parents, feeling guiltier by the minute as she persuaded them she really wanted to marry Cleveden.

Then into the family discussion walked the Duchess of Gordonstoun with Lizzie in tow. They had not liked Bath, said the duchess, accepting Lady Grant's warm welcome as if there had never been any breach in the friendship. The famous watering place had been full of provincials, went on the duchess, and so they had decided to return to London. The fact was that after only a few days at the Bath assemblies, it was evident that Lizzie would not "take." The duchess had found life a very lonely place without the friendship of Annie, Lady Grant, and therefore rushed to see her at the first opportunity after her return to London. Fiona, feeling uncomfortable in the duchess's presence, slipped from the room, murmuring an excuse. In her absence, the duchess was told of Fiona's forthcoming marriage. She gave Lady Grant her wholehearted congratulations, more grateful to her old friend for not having snubbed her than Lady Grant would ever guess. The duchess was so delighted with Lady Grant that she was even prepared to help with the arrangements for Fiona's wedding. Lizzie sat forgotten in a corner, and then she quietly left the room.

Upstairs, Fiona was regaling Christine with the whole story. "But you can't jilt a marquess!" cried Christine.

"Yes, I can," said Fiona with a laugh. "I shall collect the money for the bet. The money will no longer be needed to get Papa out of debt and so it will be all mine to do with as I wish. I could go away and take you with me, Christine. Would you like that?"

"I am going to marry Angus, if I can," said Christine.

"Of course you are, dear Christine, if that is what you want."

"It's what I want, Miss Fiona," said Christine. "But I may not be allowed to."

"Why ever not?"

"We illegitimate Grants are of the family, although not *in* the family. They like us as privileged servants, but the minute we want to marry another servant, they get hoity-toity and say we could do better. Although Angus is the piper, he's still a servant. Servants are not allowed to marry anyway."

"Then the three of us shall think of something. I can give you money so that Angus can buy a bit of land—"

"It's very kind of you," said Christine, "but Angus is a piper first and last. He would never work the land."

"Never mind. We shall contrive something. I do wish you well, Christine."

"I wish you well, too, miss. Are you sure you are not going to marry Lord Cleveden?"

"Not I," said Fiona. "I'd rather die. Thank goodness Papa has sworn to keep the money he won and never gamble again. He told me in front of Mama he'd promised her on the Bible. Of course, if he were in debt, he would probably drag me to the altar by the hair!"

"There's a noise on the landing," said Christine. She opened the door. There was no one there.

"Probably one of the maids," said Christine, shutting the door again.

The Duchess of Gordonstoun looked up as Lizzie crept quietly into the drawing room. "Where have you been?" she asked.

"I thought I'd left a fan behind when I was doing my packing," said Lizzie. "I looked in my old room, but I could not find it."

Then she meekly sat down and folded her hands in her lap and lowered her eyes as the duchess, Sir Edward, and Lady Grant went on discussing the wedding of Fiona Grant to the Marquess of Cleveden.

EIGHT

Mr. Harry Gore found he was behindhand with the gossip for the first time in his life. What made it doubly shocking to him was that such a prime piece of gossip should be about one of his closest friends. Although he affected ever afterward to have known about it all along, the announcement of the marquess's engagement to Fiona Grant came as much of a surprise to him as it did the rest of London society.

He fussed round to the marquess's town house and was ushered into that gentleman's bedroom.

"Morning, Harry," said the marquess. "What on earth has roused you from bed so early?"

"Why the news—the news of your engagement. I say, you might have told a fellow. I shall look the most utter fool."

"No one else knew beforehand, apart from the lady and her parents, and, oh, yes, the crosspatch

Duchess of Gordonstoun and that tiresome female she is puffing off. But no one else."

"But you never mentioned to *me* that you were taken with Fiona Grant!"

"Down, Harry. Down. Good boy. Sit. Have chocolate. Listen! I did not mean to propose to the lady until two nights ago and I have not seen you in the intervening time. Where have you been?"

"Out to Box Hill with the Four-in-Hand Club. I left you wholehearted and fancy free." Mr. Gore poured himself a cup of hot chocolate from a pot on a little spirit stove, raised the cup to his lips, and then put the cup down in the saucer, the chocolate untasted. "And the wedding?" he asked eagerly. "When is that to be?"

"Very soon. About ten days from now, I think."

"Ten days! Such haste. Why?"

"I am a romantic. I fear, should I wait longer, Miss Grant might change her mind."

"No lady in her right mind would jilt *you*," said Mr. Gore loyally. "There must be many disappointed ladies in London. In fact, I am not the only one the news has caused to stir early. I passed the Grant home a short time ago and witnessed the arrival on the doorstep of three young ladies, all looking extremely sour."

"Ah, yes," said the marquess. "Now, let me see. They would no doubt be Miss Euphemia Perkins, Lady Yarwood, and Miss Letitia Helmsdale."

"Goodness! You have the right of it. How?"

"A clever guess, Harry. Nothing but a clever guess."

* * *

"So, Miss Grant," Lady Yarwood was saying in chilly accents, "we have all called to offer you our felicitations and to say that we will all be here on the morrow to settle the bet."

Fiona's conscience gave her a sharp stab. She felt she should tell the ladies to forget about the bet, but her gambler's soul told her that a wager must always be paid, and besides, she badly needed the money.

"Thank you," said Fiona.

"I am to be betrothed as well," said Euphemia Perkins.

"My felicitations," said Fiona.

"Thank you," said little Miss Perkins in a hollow voice.

"So," said Fiona brightly, "that only leaves you, Letitia. Penelope is to be wed next week, before me." Penelope was Lady Yarwood.

"I have always been unlucky," mourned Letitia.

"Who is the lucky gentleman, Euphemia?" asked Fiona.

"Mr. George Delisle," said Euphemia, looking at her hands.

Penelope Yarwood and Letitia Helmsdale looked at Euphemia sympathetically. Fiona did not know this Mr. Delisle. She wondered what was wrong with him but did not like to ask.

They talked for a little about the balls and parties they were to attend, and then the three ladies rose to take their leave.

"Tell me, Fiona," said Penelope Yarwood, drawing on her gloves, "does Cleveden know about our little wager?"

"Oh, no," said Fiona.

"Mmm," murmured Penelope, looking at her thoughtfully. "You are as lucky in love as you are in your wagers. No one thought to see Cleveden drop the handkerchief."

Fiona wondered whether to tell them that she had no intention of marrying the marquess. But it seemed a heinous thing to do—to get someone to propose simply to win a bet and then jilt him.

"Tomorrow," said Fiona to herself after the ladies had left, "I shall have the money tomorrow, and then I must face Cleveden."

She felt nervous and strung up at the prospect. What would the Marquess of Cleveden be like in a rage? Angus passed the open door of the drawing room and Fiona called to him.

"Play me at hazard dice, Angus," she said when the piper came into the room.

"I haven't any money," said Angus.

"We will play for pretend money. Come, Angus. I have much on my mind and would forget my troubles."

"Very well," said Angus reluctantly. "But I have a feeling that one of these days, Miss Fiona, you will play for real stakes—and lose."

Fiona gave a superstitious shiver. If only tomorrow was over and finished with!

Fiona's game of hazard with the piper did not last very long. Sir Edward walked into the drawing room, dressed for the street. Since he had forsworn gambling, he had returned to his studies for the English bar.

He frowned awfully as he saw his daughter deftly shaking the dice and called the game to a stop.

"There will be no more gambling in the Grant household," he snapped.

"We are not playing for money," pleaded Fiona, to whom the game of dice was like a soothing drug.

"It does not matter," said Sir Edward. "Stop, now, and never let me see cards or dice played under my roof again!"

Fiona sighed and put the dice away.

"Furthermore," said Sir Edward, "as you are soon to be a married lady with your own household, I suggest you take that maid, Polly—the one you picked out of the gutter—away with you."

"Polly!" cried Fiona. "Poor child. I had almost forgot about her."

"She cannot stop stealing," said Sir Edward. "Trinkets belonging to the staff have been found under her mattress. She said she only took them to keep up her skills and meant to give them back. But she must go! And if you will not take her with you, then I shall throw her back in the kennel where she belongs."

"Send her to me, Angus," said Fiona. "Perhaps I had better see if I can put a stop to her stealing."

"And while you're about reforming the maid,"

said her father nastily, "think of reforming yourself. I am sure Cleveden does not want to lose his fortune through his wife's gambling."

"Aye," said Angus, shaking his head as Sir Edward stomped out, "there is nothing so bad as a reformed anything, be it gambler, drunkard, or lecher. They are aye harder on folks wi' their vices than someone without them would be."

Sir Edward decided to improve the state of his spleen by walking to Lincoln's Inn Fields. It was nearly noon, but the fashionable streets of the West End of London were largely deserted, society usually not rising before two in the afternoon unless something unusual had animated them, like unpaid gambling debts or the unexpected marriage announcement of a friend.

Several times he thought he heard the light patter of footsteps behind him and swung around, but there was no one to be seen.

He was walking through St. James's Park when he heard a soft voice calling his name.

Beginning to think he was being haunted, he swung about again, expecting to see no one there, but the short figure of Lizzie Grant could be clearly seen, hurrying toward him.

"Were you following me?" snapped Sir Edward as she came up to him.

"Yes," said Lizzie meekly. "I wanted to speak to you of a strange happening. I did not want to tell you in front of Fiona for she might laugh at me."

"I doubt it," said Sir Edward repressively. "Fiona is a very kind girl."

Lizzie stood in front of him, head bowed, saying nothing.

"Well?" he barked. "Out with it!"

"I don't quite know how to begin," faltered Lizzie. "I am not superstitious, but sometimes I am given to seeing signs and omens. It happened on the road back from Bath . . ."

She trailed off into silence.

"Go on," said Sir Edward, intrigued.

"I saw two magpies," said Lizzie.

"Nothing odd in that," said Sir Edward, although his gambler's heart beat a little faster. The sight of two magpies was a good omen.

"What *was* odd," said Lizzie carefully, "was that one of the magpies, the male, had a tattered tartan ribbon tied about his neck."

"What tartan was that?"

"It was the Grant tartan," said Lizzie.

Sir Edward drew in his breath in a sharp hiss. Then he tried to laugh.

"And what has some fool bird wearing a ribbon got to do with me?"

Lizzie drew closer. "The bird was in the garden of the Green Man posting house outside Marlborough where Lord Roderick Grant died in 1731."

"Gad's 'Ooonds!" cried Sir Edward. "There was the luckiest gambler of all times, and he died at a comfortable old age in that very posting house."

"It happened when I was sitting in the garden with her grace," said Lizzie. "Her grace was saying how she longed to see her dear friends,

Lady Grant and Sir Edward, when the bird hopped down at my feet."

All the old gambling fever rushed back. Sir Edward forgot his resolutions. It was a sign. An omen. The ghost of his grandfather's cousin, Lord Roderick Grant, had appeared to Lizzie so that she might let him, Sir Edward, know that Lord Roderick's ghost would be with him at the tables. He was anxious to get away.

"Most interesting, Lizzie," he forced himself to say in a casual voice.

"The duchess did not mark the bird," said Lizzie, "but you know there is a belief that we illegitimate Grants have a gift of seeing things that the ordinary person cannot."

"Yes, yes," said Sir Edward impatiently. He turned away but Lizzie caught his sleeve.

"You know you must never tell anyone what I told you," she said. "You know that."

Sir Edward did not know anything of the kind, but his superstitious Highland soul immediately told him that Lizzie was right, that his luck brought to him by this omen would fade if he told anyone.

"Yes, I know," he said. "Now I must take my leave."

He turned and strode off under the trees. Lizzie watched him go.

After he had proceeded a little way south in the direction that would take him to the Strand and then along to Lincoln's Inn Fields, Sir Edward stopped. He veered east instead—east toward St.

James's Street, east to the clubs and coffee houses.

The following afternoon, Fiona sat and awaited the arrival of her fiance, the Marquess of Cleveden. She had sent for him as soon as the three ladies had given her the money.

Fiona felt like a completely different person now that she possessed £9,000. She was no longer a weak woman who would have to marry. She was a woman of substance. Money had given her freedom.

Now all she had to do was to endure an uncomfortable interview with the marquess and then she would be free to plan her future. She knew now that what she wanted more than anything else in the world was to go home to the Highlands of Scotland. There was a small property for sale near Inverness. She would buy it, and take Angus and Christine with her. Angus must learn to work instead of lounging about, waiting for someone to ask him to play the pipes. And Polly could come too. The Highlands would cure her of thieving. There was so little to steal.

Lady Grant came into the drawing room and kissed her daughter on the cheek. "You are looking very fine, child," she said, standing back to admire Fiona's ensemble of white tunic dress ornamented with a gold key pattern.

"I am awaiting Cleveden, Mama."

"You should have told me! You cannot receive him alone before your marriage. You are allowed a few moments after the proposal but nothing after that until the wedding."

"I would rather see him alone, Mama."

"I am sorry, Fiona, I cannot allow it. What do you want to see him about?"

Fiona looked worried. She had not intended to tell her parents about breaking the engagement until it was all over.

She was about to confess the truth when Dougal, the butler, came in with the biscuits and wine she had ordered to be placed ready for the marquess's visit.

"Is Sir Edward still absent?" asked Lady Grant.

"He's been out all night, my leddy," said Dougal.

"Oh dear," moaned Lady Grant. "Surely he could not . . . he promised me . . ."

"Here's a carriage now," said Dougal.

"It will be Cleveden." Fiona ran to the window. "No, it is Papa," she said, "arriving in a hack. He looks dreadful."

They waited in silence until Sir Edward trailed miserably into the drawing room. He collapsed in a chair and buried his face in his hands.

"I've lost it all " he moaned. "Our house, our lands . . ."

Fiona took a deep breath. She would still tell Cleveden the engagement was off. But she now had money to save her home.

"Papa," she said, "I did not want to tell you this, but I won a great deal of money on a wager. Do not worry. Our lands are safe."

MISS FIONA'S FANCY

He looked up in wild hope. "How much?" he demanded.

"Nine thousand pounds," said Fiona proudly.

Down went Sir Edward's head again. "I lost fifty thousand pounds," he said.

Lady Grant screamed. She had borrowed money before to bail him out, but she did not know of anyone who could afford to lend such a vast sum. There was only the Duchess of Gordonstoun, and that lady, when appealed to before, had refused to lend a penny.

"You liar and cheat!" raged Lady Grant.

Fiona felt her world was crumbling apart. Never before had the placid and long-suffering Lady Grant given way to any strong emotion. Her mother's steadfast love for her father, faults and all, was the bedrock of Fiona's security.

Gambling does this, she thought, appalled. It wrecks souls as well as fortunes.

"The Marquess of Cleveden," announced Dougal gloomily.

The marquess strolled in and surveyed the tableau—Sir Edward sunk in a chair, Lady Grant, cheeks flaming, fists clenched, and Fiona, white and wretched.

He had not expected anything pleasant from this visit. He had fully expected Fiona to tell him the engagement was off. He had been wondering just how to handle it, for he was sure, if only he could wed Fiona, he would make her love him.

"Perhaps I should call at some other time," said the marquess.

Sir Edward looked up. He had forgotten about this rich, soon-to-be son-in-law. But the gleam of hope in his eyes quickly died. He was so disgusted with himself that the idea of presenting the marquess with such an enormous debt immediately after the marriage seemed almost worse than anything else.

"Yes, perhaps you had better go," said Fiona.

"On the other hand," said the marquess, "I might be able to help. It is all over London that you put your house and lands on the tables last night, Sir Edward."

"Do not humiliate me further," mumbled Sir Edward.

"I have no intention of humiliating you, sir. I do not wish to be saddled with a father-in-law in the Fleet Prison. I believe the sum is fifty thousand pounds."

"Yes," said Sir Edward drearily.

"I am very rich, as you know. The marriage settlemen will just cover that sum and you may have it today. But there is one condition. And that condition must remain private between myself and Miss Grant. Would you allow me a few moments alone with your daughter?"

"Yes," said Lady Grant firmly. She went across to her husband and tugged at his arm. "Come, Sir Edward," she said. "I feel that what is happening to us now is more than you deserve."

Sir Edward rose from his chair and allowed himself to be led from the room by the hand like a child.

Fiona gripped the back of a chair and faced the marquess.

"Now, Fiona," he said. "You see what comes of gambling? Before I state my conditions, I must ask you this. Have you anything to tell me?"

Those golden eyes of his bored into her own.

But Fiona could not tell him about the wager. She was sure if she did, he would cry off. It was all right for him to talk about marrying for amusement, but Fiona was sure he would not be at all amused to find out he was Miss Fiona's Fancy in a betting book. With £9,000 she could easily have told him the engagement was off. But the sum of money, which only such a short time ago had appeared so magnificent, was now only a small part of her father's staggering debt.

"No," she said miserably.

There was a short silence, and then he said, "The conditions of our marriage are this. I would have you love me for myself alone, Fiona Grant. Do not look so distressed. Call it another whim, if you will. I shall give our marriage one year. During that year, if you have not willingly, and of your own volition, come to my bed, I shall have the marriage annulled on the grounds of lack of consummation. Do you understand?"

Fiona stared at him. He saw the hope beginning to dawn in her eyes and knew that for Fiona Grant the prison gates were beginning to open. The fact that she might ever come to love him was obviously not entering her pretty head.

He felt a qualm of doubt. Was he being an arrogant fool, thinking that this Highland girl with a gambler's blood in her veins would ever come to love him? But he was a bit of a gambler himself, he thought ruefully, and Fiona Grant was worth the gamble.

"I agree," she said.

"Good," he replied as matter-of-factly as if they were two gentlemen who had just completed a business agreement.

Fiona rallied. "May I offer you some refreshment, my lord?"

"No, Fiona. You may call me Cleveden. That is the correct form. In moments of ecstasy, you may remember my name is Charles." He went forward and raised her hand to his lips.

Then he walked toward the door.

"Wait!" cried Fiona. "When shall I see you again?"

"At the altar, my sweet," he said. "Make sure you are there!"

NINE

Fiona was caught up in a maelstrom of wedding preparations. It was to be a very small, informal wedding, not held in church but in the Grants' rented London home.

Church weddings were definitely "exploded," the Duchess of Gordonstoun explained to Sir Edward and Lady Grant. Nobody who was anybody wanted to stand in some dark, drafty place making their vows. But the Grants would much have preferred the wedding to be less fashionable, and grateful as both Fiona's parents were to the marquess for saving them from ruin, the very fact that he did not want to marry their daughter in church made them worry about his character and morals, and Fiona had to endure many hours of questioning as to whether she was sure she was doing the Right Thing.

She wanted to scream that, no, she was sure she was doing the *wrong* thing, but that would mean explaining about the wager. It was of no use blaming her father for having put her in a position where she was forced to marry Lord Cleveden when she herself was just as guilty by agreeing to the engagement in the first place. To her surprise, the one question her parents did not ask her was about the £9,000 and how she had come to win such a sum.

The fact was that they had forgotten Fiona's offer, the whole episode of the marquess's proposal being remembered only in pieces and with a mixture of shame and relief.

Fiona was cured of gambling forever. She could only hope the same could be said of her father.

Up until the day before her wedding, she had never really thought of the marquess as a human being, a person with feelings. It was when she finally told Christine of the marquess's plan to annul the marriage after a year if she showed no signs of loving him that her eyes began to open.

For Christine looked amazed, and then said, "I call that handsome of him, miss. To not constrain you to any intimacy, to settle your father's debts without a murmur, surely he must be the noblest gentleman alive!"

"He is a very odd man," said Fiona cautiously, "and he did say he was marrying me because I amused him."

Christine was on the point of saying that only a man already deeply in love would behave like the marquess. But she had an instinctive feeling that that idea might frighten Fiona, and besides, Christine already had a certain loyalty to her soon-to-be employer, because Fiona was taking Christine with her to her new home until such time as she could persuade the marquess to arrange something for Christine and Angus.

So she merely cautioned, "Do be careful, Miss Fiona. Cleveden is much older than you, but there's no need to go on as if he is made of iron. He has behaved handsomely and is entitled to respect and delicacy of feeling."

"You have the right of it," sighed Fiona. "I will try to be good. Is being in love pleasant?"

"It can be heaven or hell," said Christine, "it all depends how you play your cards."

Fiona shuddered. "Don't even mention cards or dice to me again, I beg you. I must say the Duchess of Gordonstoun is doing wonders. Mama said she could not possibly manage the arrangements without her. It is even worth having that creepy Lizzie about the place."

"It is not too hard a thing to arrange a rushed wedding," said Christine dryly, "when you have unlimited funds and can command the best caterers."

"But Papa has practically no money at all now. We cannot afford it!"

"The Marquess of Cleveden has said that all accounts are to be sent to him."

"Oh, dear," sighed Fiona. "I wish he had not. I *will* try to love him, Christine, but being under such a weight of obligation makes him seem more of a parent in my eyes than a lover."

Marion Chesney

* * *

The wedding had caused a great deal of speculation and comment in society. Many tried to obtain an invitation to this curious wedding and failed. In the week before it, Mr. Harry Gore was feted and dined, for he was to be bridesman and many people wanted to be sure of a firsthand account. The odd rumor that Fiona was pregnant and therefore had to be hastily married was soon quashed energetically by Mr. Gore. He tried to find who had started the rumor, but came up against a blank wall and decided at last that probably no one person had started the malicious gossip. It was only the sort of thing that usually got about when a couple rushed to the altar.

The question most people wanted answered amused Mr. Gore. It appeared all the ladies and some of the gentlemen wanted to know if Fiona was going to wear a wedding veil. The veil had been out of fashion for a long time, being considered a primitive custom, and had only just started to come back into favor.

On the great day, Mr. Gore set out for the Grant mansion armed with a small notebook and pencil tucked away in the pocket of his tails. The man of fashion never had his pockets anywhere else but in the tails of his coat. Mr. Gore did not trust his memory and planned, during the festivities, after his duties were over, to find a quiet corner and make notes so that he could sing for his supper at all the dinners and suppers he had been invited to the following week.

Miss Fiona's Fancy

Despite the Duchess of Gordonstoun's wishes, Lizzie was not to be bridesmaid. A small six-year-old, Eileen Grant, who was on a visit to London with her parents, distant relatives of the Grants, had been chosen. She was a pretty little moppet with a head of thick red curls. Fiona was relieved not to have Lizzie's disapproving presence behind her at the ceremony, although she did feel that old stab of guilt that Lizzie's accidental birth should bar her from a position in the ceremony that would otherwise have been hers.

Shyness had made Fiona agree to wearing a veil. Her gown had been made from a ball gown, already ordered from the Misses Hatton. It had originally been a slip of white slipper satin. A train had been added and rich pearl and silver embroidery stitched over the skirt and bodice of the gown to give it a special wedding richness. A fairylike diamond tiara ornamented Fiona's head. The tiara had been loaned by the duchess, who said that although diamonds were exploded—everything that was not fashionable was said to be exploded—they were still deemed suitable for special occasions such as weddings.

The marquess resigned himself to the fact that his bride was to be piped to the makeshift altar in the drawing room by Angus.

The vicar, an old friend of the marquess's from his Oxford University days, performed the ceremony with style and affected not to hear the Duchess of Gordonstoun's remarks that a bishop would have been more in order.

Mr. Harry Gore found himself awed by the wedding couple. The bride was so very beautiful and the groom so stately in a wedding coat of blue silk embroidered with gold that the sentimental Mr. Gore found it all very moving and tried very hard not to disgrace himself by crying in the middle of the ceremony.

Fiona had not rehearsed the ceremony with the marquess because he had been too busy at the House of Lords to spare any time before the wedding, but her parents had schooled her well and she made her responses in a clear firm voice.

None of the fright at taking such a monumental step appeared in her eyes. As most of the servants were members of the Clan Grant, the festivities after the wedding were a very democratic affair, with the servants dancing with the lords and ladies. Mr. Gore thought it all very charming and entered into the spirit of the thing by leading a kitchen maid onto the floor for a Scottish reel.

It was perhaps unfortunate that Polly should have been allowed to come into contact with so many jewels and fine silk handkerchiefs, but Christine and Angus took her out into the hall before the guests left, and "shook her down," as Angus put it, and returned the valuables to the guests.

It was only when she was up in her room, looking at her corded trunks and waiting for Christine to put the finishing touches to her carriage dress, that Fiona began to panic. She had not stopped to think, she realized, anytime during the past week of all that this marriage entailed. She might never see her home in the Highlands again. She was going off alone with this new husband, a strange man, who, despite his kindness to her parents, had shown a liking for slums and sleazy masquerades at the Pantheon.

There had been a waltz during the festivities and he had held her too close. The feel of his hard body against her own had done very uncomfortable things to Fiona. There was a whole world of sexual relationships between men and women she did not understand and of which she was becoming increasingly afraid.

Christine looked at her tense face and said gently, "I shall be with you, my lady. My lord is a man of honor. He will do nothing to upset you."

"Are you sure, Christine? I do not even know where we are going."

"To Lord Cleveden's town house. He plans to take you on a honeymoon much later."

Fiona sighed. "I never even thought to ask," she marveled. "At least you will be with me, Christine. I do not think I could bear it otherwise."

She put her arms about the maid and Christine held her close.

"If it does not work out," said Christine softly, "you have only a year of marriage to endure. Only a year. And then somehow we will find the way home."

The marquess's town house was in Curzon Street. His staff was waiting in the hall to greet her. Fiona was introduced to them all, and knew she would find it hard to adjust to living with these correct and formal servants after living in the company of easygoing Highland ones.

The wedding celebrations had gone on until late in the evening and so the question of *bed* loomed large in Fiona's mind. The room that had been prepared for her was very much the room of the lady of the house. There was a vast double bed, but it was draped with a canopy of white lace. The furniture was delicate and feminine, and large vases of flowers scented the air.

Christine prepared her mistress for bed. "Do not worry, my lady, they have given me a room next door to yours. You have only to call out if you need me."

"Address me as Fiona when we are alone together. I would have liked a sister like you, Christine."

"Then we shall be sisters in private," said Christine. "Sit down and let me brush your hair."

Fiona sat down at the toilet table. Her green eyes, shadowed and wary, looked back at her from the glass. Her nightgown, a miracle of lace and fine muslin, was as finely fashioned as any ball gown and almost as elaborate.

The door opened and the marquess walked in. Christine stopped brushing Fiona's hair, curtsied, and then stood to attention.

The marquess was wearing a silk dressing gown over a nightgown and his bare feet were thrust into red morocco slippers.

Miss Fiona's Fancy

"Leave us, Christine," he said, softening the order with a smile.

Christine curtsied again and withdrew. She went to her own room and softly closed the door. She wondered whether to listen at the door in case Fiona needed help and then decided against it. Fiona was a married woman now, and the marquess was her husband. Christine undressed quickly, plunged into her narrow bed, and pulled the pillows over her ears.

The marquess sat down in a chair beside the fire and surveyed his bride.

"Come and sit down, my love," he said. "Would you like something to drink before you retire?"

"Oh, yes, please," said Fiona dismally. She was sure he did not mean to keep his promise, that he meant to share her bed.

"And what would you like? Warm milk?"

"No, wine, I think."

The marquess rang the bell and then ordered a footman to bring wine and glasses.

Fiona sat down opposite him, blushing a little because she was only wearing a nightdress and mentally telling herself not to be silly, that the nightdress was less revealing than most of the fashions one wore during the day.

"That went off well, I think," said the marquess, stifling a yawn. "Very energetic family you come from, my love. All those wild dances! I saw that peculiar cousin of yours, Lizzie Grant, was present, very finely gowned, too. Now there is someone I do not wish you to have anything to do with."

"I agree gladly to that," said Fiona, "for I cannot like her."

"Now, as to the matter of your servants . . ."

"Do not ask me to dismiss Christine," said Fiona, appalled.

"No, no," he said soothingly. "But do you remember that waif, Polly, that you rescued? I am afraid my butler and housekeeper have taken a dislike to her after only a few minutes in her company."

"She *is* difficult," said Fiona. "Let me see her tomorrow and I shall try to make her behave better."

"I doubt it. Here is our wine." He dismissed the footman and poured her a glass and then watched as Fiona drank the contents in one gulp. He gently took the glass from her and said, "You have no reason to wish Dutch courage this night, my sweeting. Now, as to the matter of Christine. She bears the same name as you."

"She is what we call an 'accidental daughter,'" said Fiona. "Christine is very dear to me."

"So I have noticed. Do you have many such accidents in your family? I suppose it is the long northern winters that are at fault. I suppose your relatives have nothing better to do."

"At least they acknowledge their accidents," said Fiona.

"As to Christine's future . . ."

"I meant to ask you about that," said Fiona

hurriedly. "Christine is in love with our piper, Angus Robertson. I hope to be able to settle them someday."

"Why the piper?" groaned the marquess. "Anyone else I would gladly have admitted to my household. For the year of our trial marriage, I suggest you elevate Christine to the position of your companion. Lady's maids are easily found. After the year is up, we will discuss her future."

"Thank you," said Fiona.

"Tell me about your home in Scotland," he said abruptly.

And Fiona did—shyly at first until she warmed to her subject, not knowing she was betraying a great deal of aching homesickness.

The marquess watched her carefully, plotting his next move.

When she had finished, he thought, I could cope with a human rival better. 'Tis hard to have to compete with a home. But he said aloud, "Fiona, I am going to be a great deal occupied for some weeks with my affairs in London and then I must travel to Gloucester to put my estates in order. Would you like to visit your home? You may take that wretched piper away with you and leave him there. And the thieving Polly."

"Oh, my lord," said Fiona, tears of gratitude spilling out of her eyes.

"Don't cry," he said softly. "Your eyes are so green, I am amazed to see your tears are like crystal. I would have expected pure emeralds to drop from them."

Fiona tugged a small handkerchief out of the sleeves of her nightgown and gave her nose a vigorous blow.

He watched her with tender amusement. "You may leave in a week's time. Of course society will tattle and assume we have quarreled, but I never paid any attention to what anyone said in the past and I do not mean to start now. Talk to that Polly creature tomorrow and warn her if she continues to thieve, then she may not go with you but will be returned to the streets."

"Yes, my lord."

"Yes, *Charles*."

"Yes, Charles."

He got to his feet. "Then good night, Fiona."

Fiona turned and looked at the bed and then at the marquess. "You mean you are not going to . . . to . . .—"

"Not until the decision is yours. I am sure I can keep my slavering masculine lusts in check for a little longer."

Fiona rose and curtsied. "Good night, Charles. And, oh, *thank you*."

"You may kiss me, if that is not too much to ask," he teased.

No longer afraid of him, Fiona went straight into his arms. The kiss was firm and warm and comforting.

When he drew away, he smiled at her and said, "Nothing to alarm you in that, was there?"

"Oh, no," said Fiona innocently. "I shall kiss you again, if you wish."

"Tomorrow," he said. "Perhaps tomorrow."

He went out and closed the door. Too excited to sleep, Fiona burst into Christine's room to tell her the news. They chattered on excitedly into the night, and the marquess, sitting reading in his room along the corridor, heard the murmurs of voices, sighed, and wondered whether a year was long enough for his wife to grow up.

Fiona did not see her husband the next morning and experienced an odd feeling of disappointment to find he had left early for the House of Lords. But her parents called and were excited to learn of her proposed visit north, seeing nothing odd in the fact that a newly wed man should wish to send his bride away so soon. Sir Edward confessed to homesickness but said he hoped to complete his studies soon, and if he saw no prospect of clients, he would cut his losses by returning to the north himself.

They had only just left when the next callers arrived—the Duchess of Gordonstoun and Lizzie.

Fiona tried her best to be friendly and welcoming but she hoped they would not stay long. Her news of her forthcoming journey to the Highlands met with a different reception. The duchess asked anxiously if she had done anything to give Cleveden a disgust of her and looked disbelieving when Fiona said they were on the best of terms. Fiona noticed with irritation a small secret smile on Lizzie's face and knew that Lizzie at least was not convinced that all was well and was enjoying the thought.

Then Lizzie murmured something to the duchess, who looked sharply at Christine, who was sitting sewing in a corner.

"Why is your maid seated?" demanded the duchess. "She should remain standing in your presence."

"Christine is no longer my maid," said Fiona with a smile. "My lord has elevated her to the position of companion."

"How odd!" exclaimed the duchess, staring rudely at Christine. "But then the whims of the English aristocracy have always baffled me."

Fiona thought she surprised a flash of envy and dislike in Lizzie's eyes as they looked at Christine, but the next moment, Lizzie's expression was as meek and colorless as usual. She had told the marquess she would not have anything to do with Lizzie, but she could hardly forbid the girl the house when she came on a social call with the duchess.

Fiona tried not to show her relief when the duchess took her leave.

Then she sent Christine to fetch Polly and read that young maid a stern lecture.

Polly wept and promised to be good. She wept again when she was told she was to accompany her mistress north, and it transpired between sobs that Polly was convinced she was being taken away to a savage barbaric land from which she would never return.

After soothing and reassuring Polly, Fiona went out walking with Christine, only to find on her return that the elegant downstairs saloon of the marquess's town house was full of curious callers waiting to greet the new marchioness.

The following days were taken up with receiving and making calls. The marquess seemed to be nowhere about during the day and Fiona often sat up late until she heard him mount the stairs and go to his room. He never came to see her and she began to wonder if he had indeed taken a dislike to her.

On the eve of her departure, she could not bear it any longer, and she made her way to his room and shyly scratched at the door.

A deep voice called. "Enter," and Fiona went in.

Her lord was lying in a large four-poster bed, a book on his lap.

Those odd yellow-gold eyes of his surveyed her curiously.

"I am delighted to see you," he said. "What is the reason for this late-night visit?"

"I am to leave in the morning," said Fiona, "and I have seen nothing of you."

He looked amused. "I was sure that would have delighted you."

"Not really," said Fiona. "It feels very odd to be married and yet to see nothing of one's husband."

"I shall have plenty of time for you when you return," he said. "Do not be away too long."

"I shall miss you," said Fiona politely.

"My dear child, you cannot miss someone you do not even know. Be off with you and have a good night's sleep."

Fiona hesitated. "I shall kiss you good-bye," she said bravely, advancing on the bed.

"As you wish." He held out his arms.

Fiona sank down on the bed beside him and raised her lips, hoping to convey by the warmth of her kiss all the gratitude she felt toward him.

At first, his kiss was like the previous two, firm and impersonal. Then his lips softened and moved against her own and his arms tightened about her. Fiona clutched his shoulders like a drowning woman as a wave of passion engulfed her. Her body seemed to fuse with his own, although the blankets were between them. His passion was making her body wanton, making it move languorously and provocatively against his.

Then he put her away from him and said, "Good night, Fiona. I shall see you tomorrow before you leave."

She rose shakily from the bed, looking at him with wide dazed eyes.

"Good night," he said again.

Fiona went out and closed the door. "It will be all right," she said to herself. "I have nothing to worry about. I am going home."

But a small niggling thought came into her

brain, a thought that kept her awake during the night.

Her husband was a handsome and virile man, and London was full of beautiful women, women who would be only too happy to keep him amused in her absence!

TEN

Fiona sat in the swaying traveling carriage three months later, looking sadly at the empty seat opposite where Christine should have been sitting, and thinking her life would never be quite the same again.

Unlike that last leisurely journey south with her parents, this one was to be completed in the shortest time possible. Fiona and her servants rose early and traveled until night fell.

She ran over in her mind the shocks and disappointments of her visit. First, her home, Strathglass House, had seemed very shabby for the first time. The London servants had complained bitterly of hard cold beds and smoking fires. Battles had raged between them and the Highland servants, for the Highland servants of the lower orders would not observe distinctions of rank.

Gradually, to Fiona's relief, they seemed to have come to some sort of truce and the stiff English servants had begun to unbend and to adopt the free and easy manners of the Highlanders.

Then Angus had been offered the post of piper to a Highland chieftain in Cromarty. His new job meant he would have a cottage on the estate and be allowed to wed Christine. The job did not involve any work other than piping.

Fiona longed to beg Christine to stay with her and yet fell silent before the happiness on her companion's face. Also, she knew that although her father was more free and easy in his ways than most, he still disapproved of servants marrying. She traveled to Cromarty to attend Christine and Angus's wedding and felt very lonely when she returned to Strathglass alone. Her lady's maid, Mary, was correct, polite and English, and good at her job. But of what use, thought Fiona, were the latest modes and hairstyles when there was no one to see them? It took some time before she realized that by no one she meant her absent husband. The memory of that passionate kiss grew stronger and stronger as the days passed. Still, Fiona clung to her old home.

And then one day, Polly, who had become her faithful shadow, disappeared. The servants said that a band of tinkers, Highland gypsies, had come to the kitchen door, offering to mend pots. Polly had fallen into conversation with their leader, a swarthy, dirty-looking man. The next the servants had known was that Polly was riding off on the back of this man's horse without even turning back to shout farewell.

Fiona would not believe them. She became convinced Polly had been abducted. She called together her father's regiment and marched out in search of the tinkers. They found Polly in a gypsy encampment outside Fort Augustus at the end of Loch Ness. She was dirty, happy, and unrepentant. She told Fiona she had gone through a Scotch marriage with the leader—a marriage made by two people simply announcing to the world at large that they are married—and that she had never been so happy—not ever.

There was nothing Fiona could do but ride off and leave her and apologize to her father's men for having made them go out on such a long and weary search.

She was in no mood to speak to Jamie Grant, whom she found waiting for her on her return, and a very petulant Jamie at that. It appeared that Jamie had considered himself as good as betrothed to Fiona and insisted on acting the part of the jilted lover. He ranted and raged and then demanded, "And who *is* this Englishman? How can he compare to the likes o' me?"

And Fiona, looking at Jamie's sulky, boyish face, at his grubby kilt, at his posturing ways, remembered with an ache at her heart her husband's elegant bearing and charming manner.

She had left him! And for so long!

After Jamie had stormed his way out, Fiona issued orders for their departure south.

Now, with rain smearing the carriage windows, she thought the journey would never end. Had her sophisticated and elegant husband taken a mistress? So many men did, and shortly after they were married, too. She had wasted part of her precious trial year of marriage by journeying to Scotland.

Fiona wished she had Christine with her to talk to. Christine would have reassured her, would have told her the marquess was not the man to flaunt a mistress. But now there was only silent Mary, the lady's maid, who would not consider it her place to comfort and advise on any subject.

More weary days of travel passed. Fiona ached in every limb, for although the carriage was well sprung, some of the roads were so rough that she had been thrown from side to side for hours.

And then at last they topped Highgate Hill and the end of the long, weary road was in sight.

Fiona kept pulling out a mirror from her reticule and studying her face anxiously. She wanted to look her best. How would he greet her? Would he kiss her?

By the time the carriage rolled to a stop in front of the elegant house in Curzon Street, Fiona was trembling with anticipation. She did not wait for the groom to let down the carriage steps but jumped down and ran to the door.

The door was opened by Osborne, the butler. "Where is my lord?" cried Fiona, running past him into the hall.

"He is at his club, my lady," said Osborne, "and not expected home until late."

Fiona was about to demand that a servant be

sent to the club to let her lord know of her arrival home, but she was overcome with a wave of shyness and thought he might be annoyed to be so summoned by his wife-in-name-only.

She went upstairs and changed into a modish gown of green silk, one she had not worn before. It had a matching pelisse held at the front with gold frogging. She told her exhausted maid to go to bed but she herself went downstairs to wait for the marquess's arrival home.

No sooner was she seated than Osborne entered to announce Mrs. Henry Buxtable, Miss Euphemia Perkins, and Miss Letitia Helmsdale.

"How did you know I was back?" exclaimed Fiona as the three ladies were ushered in. "I have but shortly arrived in Town."

"We were having a council of war over ices at Gunter's when we saw your carriage drive past," said Penelope Buxtable, the former Lady Yarwood.

"It is wonderful to see you," said Fiona, although the unexpected presence of the three who had taken part in the wager made her feel decidedly uncomfortable. She rang for tea and cakes and talked about her journey. The three listened silently and Fiona had a feeling they were waiting for the servants to serve tea and depart before they got down to the real reason for their visit. There was a very determined air about all of them.

And so it was. No sooner had the door closed behind the butler and footmen than Penelope interrupted Fiona's dissertation on the state of the

English roads by saying harshly, "You've got to help us."

"I?" said Fiona. "I shall most certainly help you if I can."

"You had better," said Penelope bleakly. "For if you don't, we shall tell Cleveden of that wager."

"You would not!" cried Fiona, horrified. Ever afterward, she wondered why she had not spiked their guns by telling them a lie and saying that Cleveden already knew.

"Oh, yes, we would," said Penelope. "We are all in a pickle. I am in love—"

"But you have only been married such a short time," said Fiona, distressed.

"I did not then know what love was," said Penelope. Her harsh features softened. "That was before I met Peregrine Finlay."

"Who is this . . . ?"

"A very beautiful poet who loves me to distraction. You shall meet him. We are tired of snatching odd moments at balls and theaters. We shall now meet here—in your home. It is well known that Cleveden is always out and about."

"And if I do not allow this arrangement, you will tell Cleveden about the bet?"

"Yes."

Fiona turned to the other two. "And do you also wish to use my home for assignations?" she asked bitterly.

"You are now a marchioness," said Euphemia, looking distressed but determined. "You are an important member of the *ton*. My parents are forcing me to marry Mr. George Delisle, who is old and horrible."

"But your parents are rich," said Fiona.

"Papa thinks a man of his own age is more suited to be my husband. But I have fallen in love with a certain Captain Peter Gaunt. You must help us."

Fiona shook her head in bewilderment. "And you?" She asked Letitia Helmsdale.

"I *want* a husband, any husband," said Letitia. "I have a good dowry but I am sadly plain. Mama and Papa are older than most parents and their circle of friends is equally old and staid. I do not take at balls and parties and need to be introduced to young men. *You* will soon know many eligible members of the *ton*. The Little Season is soon upon us. I wish you to sponsor me, Fiona."

"I can agree to that," said Fiona. She turned to the other two. "But what you ask is impossible. Penelope, I cannot allow my husband's home to be used for your meetings, and you, poor Euphemia, I really don't see what I can do."

"You must think of something," said the normally timid Euphemia mulishly. "I shall call on you early tomorrow, eleven in the morning, say, to discuss the matter further."

"And I," said Penelope harshly, "shall call on you at three in the afternoon. Peregrine will call as well. You may entertain us for a few moments and then leave us alone."

"But what if Cleveden is here!" exclaimed Fiona.

"Then you must get rid of him," said Penelope sternly.

A carriage rolled to a stop outside. Fiona ran to the window. "It is Cleveden!" she said. She turned and looked pleadingly at her three companions.

Three pairs of eyes as hard as Scottish pebbles stared back.

"Do we tell him, or do you agree to help us?" said Penelope.

"Oh, yes, yes, *yes*," said Fiona, quite distracted. She was pushing them toward the door when her husband walked in.

"My love!" he said. "Here you are, newly arrived after an exhausting journey and already fatiguing yourself with entertaining. But do not let me hurry you off, ladies. Do stay, I beg you."

"No, Cleveden," said Penelope, drawing on her gloves. "We were on the point of leaving when you arrived."

"I have not introduced you, Cleveden," said Fiona. "May I present—"

"I am already acquainted with these ladies," said the marquess. He made them his best bow, and flashing meaningful glances at Fiona, the ladies took their leave.

Fiona sank into a chair and stared miserably at the fire.

"Well?" he demanded softly. "Is this all the welcome I am to expect?"

"No, Cleveden," said Fiona, springing up and rushing into his arms. "It is only that I am so tired."

His arms closed about her and he held her close.

Fiona longed to burst into tears and tell him everything. But she dared not. She was afraid of losing him, afraid of losing this man she had married, this man with whom she had suddenly tumbled head over heels in love.

"Entertaining the three witches is enough to exhaust anyone," he said. "Is there anything you would like to tell me, Fiona?"

She could sense him waiting for her reply, sense his whole body waiting.

But she could not tell him about the wager. "No, Cleveden," she said sadly.

"No, Charles."

"No, Charles," echoed Fiona in a hollow voice.

"Then let us have dinner and you can tell me all about your visit to your home."

During dinner he studied his wife's expressive face. She talked quite gaily about the journey, and then cried a little as she told him about Christine's marriage and about runaway Polly, and then brightened again as she described the beauty of the Highlands, and magnificent sunsets, the purple heather blazing on the flanks of the steep mountains, but from time to time a shadow would cross her eyes and she would fall silent and he would have to prompt her to go on.

After dinner, she looked so weary, he told her to go to bed.

He kissed her on the forehead. Fiona looked up at him, her lips now aching for his kiss. "What of you?" she asked.

"I am not tired," he said. "I think I shall look for Harry Gore. He is such an amusing rattle and is just recently returned to Town."

The marquess ran his friend to earth at Mr. Gore's cramped lodgings in Jermyn Street.

Mr. Gore hailed him with delight and, in his usual way, demanded to know all the gossip of society.

"You know me, Harry," laughed the marquess, "I rely on *you* to keep me abreast on what's going on. I think some slightly dated gossip will suffice. You have only been out of Town for two weeks. Now, tell me what you know about the following three ladies—Mrs. Henry Buxtable, Miss Euphemia Perkins, and Miss Letitia Helmsdale."

Mr. Gore was busy unpacking one of his trunks, having sent his man out to buy supper from one of the coffee houses. He sat back on his heels and looked up at the marquess.

"Any use my asking you why you are interested in those three."

"No."

"I thought not. What a cagey fellow you are! Well, the former Lady Yarwood, now Mrs. Henry Buxtable, thinks she is having a discreet affair with Peregrine Finlay, a tiresome poet. The only person, apart from yourself, who does not seem to know is her excellent husband. Colonel Henry is one of those stern, silent sorts who would call out anyone who dared to malign his wife, so no one tells him. I do not think the guilty couple have gone further than squeezing hands. I do not think

Peregrine capable of going further, but he thinks it enhances his reputation as a man about town to appear to have an affair with a married lady. The colonel loves his wife, a fact silly Peregrine has not taken into account. Odd. Mrs. Buxtable looks just like a horse, but then the colonel is fond of horses."

"Go on, my malicious friend, what of the other two?"

"There is the sad tale of little Miss Perkins. Her parents have forced her to become engaged to George Delisle, who is a horrible man and practically old enough to be her grandfather. But these sort of marriages happen all the time and there is nothing one can do to stop them. Miss Helmsdale—nothing. Not a whisper of gossip. One of the last Season's failures. Good dowry but no takers. Parents don't know how to puff her off and don't do the groundwork. So there you are. Nothing really out of the way. When does your beautiful marchioness return?"

"She is returned. This evening."

"And you not by her side!"

"My poor wife is exhausted and is already asleep."

"In that case, stay and share my modest supper—chops and porter."

"No, I thank you. I dined earlier. I shall share a bottle of wine with you and then return."

An hour later, the marquess climbed the stairs to his bedroom. He was opening his bedroom door when he had a feeling he was being watched. He swung around and raised his candle. Fiona was standing at the doorway of her room, looking at him sadly.

"What! Still awake, my sweet?" he said.

"I could not sleep," said Fiona.

"Then come and talk to me."

Fiona came slowly along the passage as the marquess entered his bedroom and dismissed his valet who was laying out his nightclothes by saying, "No, Gustave, I shall put myself to bed."

Wearing her nightgown and wrapper, Fiona sat in a chair by the fire. The marquess took off his coat and started to unwind his cravat.

"I had better leave," said Fiona. "You are undressing."

"Stay. You are my wife. There is nothing so shocking about me taking off my clothes. I am not deformed."

Fiona, who had half risen from her seat, sat down again.

He undressed quickly and then went to the toilet table and splashed water over himself and then scrubbed himself down with a towel. Fiona tried to look away but found her eyes drawn to the play of muscles under the smooth skin of his back. Her breath came quickly and her skin felt hot and prickly under the thin muslin of her gown.

He dragged a nightshirt on over his head and then faced her. "I would have thought you would be exhausted," he said.

"I did sleep a little," faltered Fiona. "But I had bad dreams."

"Then come and lie with me, my love. I shall only hold you until you sleep."

He climbed into bed and pulled back the blankets on the other side.

"Come!" he ordered.

Still clutching her wrapper tightly about her, Fiona shyly climbed into bed.

He pulled her into his arms and held her against the length of his body.

"Now, sleep!" he said.

He must be mad! thought Fiona. How could she sleep with her heart doing somersaults in her chest, with her breasts becoming hard and swollen, and with the searing memory of that one passionate kiss hardly ever out of her mind?

"Are you cold?" he asked softly. "You are shivering. I shall warm you."

He began to stroke her back.

"Oh, *no*," moaned Fiona. The stroking stopped immediately.

She propped herself up on one elbow and looked down at him. She was about to tell him she could endure no more and must leave. One kiss, mocked her mind, one kiss and *then* leave.

He looked up into her eyes and then his own began to blaze.

"No," he muttered. "It must come from you, Fiona. I told you I would never bed an unwilling wife."

She fell across his chest, and with a little sob, her searching lips found his.

What ensued was more like a battle than tender romance as the marquess released all the passion he felt for her and got it back in full measure from this Highland girl who had never been taught that ladies should lie back and endure it all passively. The blankets ended up on the floor along with their torn and tumbled nightclothes. The marquess's old four-poster bed, which had been his grandfather's, creaked and rocked like some storm-tossed ship riding out a gale. He had tried to warn her it would hurt, but the passionate creature in his arms seemed to relish everything and cry for more.

Finally, as they tired and their lovemaking became more sensuous, more languorous, his questing hand stilled the wanton body under him and he asked softly, "You are sure that nothing troubles you, my darling Fiona? There is nothing you could tell me now that could stop me loving you."

But Fiona only buried her head in his chest and would not reply.

At last, when she fell asleep, the marquess stroked her hair tenderly and said, "Trust is all I need now, Fiona. A little trust from you and I will be assured you love me for myself alone and not for my fortune. Then I shall count myself the happiest man in England."

His love gave a gentle, if unromantic, snore. He smiled and cradled her in his arms and then he, too, fell asleep.

ELEVEN

The sound of her husband washing awoke Fiona. She struggled up against the pillows. "What time is it, Charles?" she asked sleepily.

"Nearly eleven. Go back to sleep. I have an appointment with someone, but I shall return quite soon and then we shall take a pleasant drive somewhere."

Fiona scrambled out of bed and clutched the ruin of her nightdress to her naked body.

"I had forgot, Charles," she said miserably, "Euphemia Perkins is to call at eleven."

"Then you will be shot of her by the time I return."

"But Penelope, Mrs. Buxtable, is to call at three!"

He turned away from her and studied his face in the mirror. "Then I shall help you get rid of her."

"No, you mustn't do that!" said Fiona. "She wishes to talk to me about . . . about female things."

"Then I shall make sure you are left alone with her."

"I should really have much preferred to have gone driving with you," said Fiona, feeling wretched.

"In that case, maybe the fairies will grant your wish and something will happen to make Penelope disappear."

"I must dress," said Fiona. "Euphemia will be here in a few moments."

He walked over to her and held her naked hips. "Shall we send Euphemia away?" he said softly.

"No, no," gabbled Fiona. "And you have an appointment, Charles." A hard look crossed his face and Fiona looked at him pleadingly.

He looked down at her worried eyes and relented. "Go," he said, giving her a little push.

Fiona dropped her tattered nightgown, seized the coverlet from the bed, and, wrapping it about her, ran to her own room.

She dressed very quickly, and then rushed downstairs in time to meet Euphemia, who had just arrived.

Euphemia, as soon as they were alone, poured out her woes.

"Does this Captain Gaunt have any money?" asked Fiona.

"Not very much," said Euphemia. "But he says

we could live in a modest way—very modest."

"And have you no money of your own?"

"I have a small income from a trust from my grandmother. But what is the use? I am now seventeen, but still too young to be independent. My parents would never allow me to marry and I need their consent."

"Then go to Gretna Green!" cried Fiona. "No one can stop you marrying there! You do not need your parents' consent for a Gretna marriage."

"But we do not have a traveling carriage. I mean, the captain does not have one."

"Then *rent* one," said Fiona impatiently.

"Captain Gaunt is not very good at arranging things," said Euphemia, hanging her head.

"Goodness! How old is this captain?"

"He is twenty."

"How does he expect to lead his men if he cannot even arrange a traveling carriage? Oh, do not look so miserable, Euphemia. I shall hire it for you. When can you leave?"

"Captain Gaunt wrote to me from his regiment in Shropshire. He is due to start a month's leave next week."

Fiona heard her husband moving about upstairs. "I shall hire a carriage for—let me see, this is the tenth—for the seventeenth. I shall call for you as if it is a social visit—"

"No, you cannot do that!" squeaked Euphemia. "My parents do not know I am here. I was told to have nothing more to do with you."

"Why, pray?"

Euphemia hung her head. "I needed to explain to them why I wanted three thousand pounds. I told them you ran a gambling hell."

"Oh, my poor reputation!" moaned Fiona. "Then tell this captain to call for me here. I shall find some way to get rid of Cleveden on the afternoon of the seventeenth. Tell Captain Gaunt to attend me here at three o'clock. Can you leave your house without your maid?"

"No, but she is very loyal to me and will come with me. She is here now, waiting in the hall."

"Then come here as well!"

"But only imagine if we should be seen leaving together!"

"Very well. Hire a postchaise and take it to Barnet and wait at the top of the hill. I shall drive off with the captain myself and pick you up there and then return to Town after I have safely seen you on your way."

"Oh, Fiona," said Euphemia, beginning to cry, "I am so grateful to you. You are so resolute."

"I am only doing all this under duress," said Fiona dryly. She heard her husband's step on the stairs. "Go quickly, Euphemia, and not a word of this to anyone!"

The marquess entered and looked curiously at the red-eyed Euphemia, who bobbed him a curtsy as she left the room.

He raised an eyebrow at his wife, but Fiona said

in a colorless voice, "A trifling problem, Charles. Euphemia is easily overset."

He glanced at the window. "Here comes your parents, my love. I must escape or I will never be on time for that appointment."

He did not kiss her and Fiona felt worried. How could she have done such a thing as plan an elopement? If only she could unburden herself to her husband. But he would think she had only married him for his money and he would never believe she loved him.

Sir Edward and Lady Grant came in and Fiona was able to relax somewhat as she answered their eager questions about Strathglass House and its neighbors. But as they were preparing to go Sir Edward said, "Fiona, I would be careful of that Lizzie girl. I am not quite sure whether she is stupid or malicious."

"How so, Papa?"

"Although I have not gambled since that terrible time when I was rescued by Cleveden's marriage settlement, it has been hard for me. I see a hunchback, or magpies, or a rainbow, and the old longing comes back.... Do you understand?"

"Yes, Papa. Although I myself have resolved never to gamble again, I find it hard to keep to my resolution. Sometimes something seems like a lucky sign or omen."

"Exactly. Now, before my last gambling bout, Lizzie waylaid me in St. James's Park and told me that on the road from Bath she had seen two magpies in the garden of the Green Man. One bird, she said, had a tattered ribbon 'round its neck and that ribbon was of the Grant tartan. Now, as you know, Lord Roderick Grant died there, so it seemed to me as if the ghost of that lucky gambler had come back to me through Lizzie."

Fiona gave a superstitious shiver. "Perhaps she did see such a bird, Papa."

"Only wait! T'other day, Lizzie came with Betty —the Duchess of Gordonstoun—and Betty was congratulating me on my reformed ways. When I set out for Lincoln's Inn Fields, once more Lizzie contrived to follow me. She said she had been walking along Clarges Street and she had seen the ghost of Charles James Fox."

Charles James Fox, who had died only a few years before at his home in Clarges Street, had been not only a famous politician and champion of the American Colonies in their fight for independence but a notorious gambler.

"She said," Sir Edward went on, "that the ghost had handed her a playing card, the queen of hearts, and disappeared. Lizzie gave me the playing card, saying she felt sure the ghost meant it for me. My heart beat fast and I was rushing off to the tables, for the old fever was burning in my blood, when I met a lawyer friend who knew of my Fatal Tendency. I told him I was going to the club, and when he tried to stop me, I told him Lizzie's story. He laughed in my face. In a fury, I showed him the playing card, and he laughed even harder. The playing card, he said, was manufactured by Bartholomew, who had only started in business two years ago. So, he pointed out, it was very odd that a ghost should have handed Lizzie a card from a modern pack. Perhaps Lizzie thought she saw something. Perhaps she makes up stories to feel important, but there is a thought in my mind that she might have done it deliberately."

Fiona sat in silence while she thought hard. Then she said, "You know, Papa, once when I was telling Christine I would rather do anything than marry Cleveden—do not look so worried, I was only funning—Christine thought she heard someone outside my bedroom door. There was no one there when she looked, but Lizzie was in our home that day and Lizzie might guess that were you in deep debt, then you would force me to accept Cleveden's hand. I think she hates me and yet I cannot guess the reason. I have never done her any harm."

Fiona felt she was only telling a mild lie by saying she was joking about Cleveden with Christine. She certainly did not want her parents to remember the wager.

Lady Grant sighed. "Charles, her father, never would have anything to do with her. She was brought up in his household but treated always as a servant's child. We never could find out the name of Lizzie's mother. Charles is a close-mouthed bitter man."

"Her situation is an awkward one," said Fiona.

"But I will go carefully. Cleveden does not want me to have anything to do with her."

But her parents had only been gone for half an hour when Osborne announced the arrival of Lizzie Grant. She tripped lightly in, holding out both hands in welcome.

"Where is the duchess?" asked Fiona.

"She is still asleep."

"I hope you did not come unescorted."

"Oh, no," said Lizzie proudly, "I have my own personal maid. She is waiting outside."

"Why are you come?" asked Fiona curiously.

"To pay my respects," said Lizzie with a little laugh. "Also, I was worried about you, dear Fiona. All London was amazed when your husband sent you packing so soon after the wedding."

"My husband did not send me packing, Lizzie, so if you are here to ferret out gossip about an unhappy marriage, I must tell you you are set for disappointment. I love my husband very much and we are very happy."

"Oh, Fiona. So hard! That you should misunderstand my concern."

"I do not trust you, Lizzie," said Fiona. "I do not wish to see you again. The Duchess of Gordonstoun is a friend of the family, and if you come with her, then I shall be obliged to see you. I know now you were the one who tricked Papa into gambling and tried to trick him again. Why?"

Lizzie sat with lowered eyes. Fiona waited

wearily for a burst of tears and protestations of innocence. But when Lizzie raised her eyes, they were bright with malice.

"And how goes the Marquess of Cleveden?" asked Lizzie. "How goes Miss Fiona's Fancy?"

"So you know," said Fiona evenly. "Now, get out!"

"Not before I have finished," said Lizzie. "I am not your faithful lapdog like Christine to bow before *you* because of *my* bastard status. Why should you be pampered and petted and I neglected?"

"One could hardly say you were neglected. The duchess nearly ruined my chances of marriage in her efforts to put you first."

"What else should my own mother do?"

"Your *mother*!"

"Yes."

"This is another of your tales," said Fiona. "When I first met you, I could swear the duchess was meeting you for the first time as well."

"Almost." Lizzie sneered. "Quite wild in her youth was Mama. After bearing me, she handed me over to Lord Charles and the only subsequent interest she took in me was to write to him when I was fifteen and suggest I be sent to London and put to a trade. But when she saw me again, her natural maternal affections came to the fore-although she hid them as well as she has hidden the secret of my birth. Once you were engaged to Cleveden, she did not try to put a spoke in your wheel, for, as she said, 'He would have been better to have married you, my dear, but Cleveden is too much a man of the world and would soon have found out about your illegitimate status. You, dear Lizzie, will need to be content with some less important gentleman.' I know your father's debts forced you to marry Cleveden as well as that stupid bet. I know I brought that about. I hope you are unhappy, Fiona. I hope Cleveden *beats* you. It would do you good to learn what it is to be mocked and slighted."

"I am not responsible for your accident of birth," said Fiona.

"The whole world is unjust," said Lizzie. "I am trying to even the score through you."

She is mad! thought Fiona with a shiver. She rang the bell.

"Osborne," she said faintly, "show Miss Grant out."

When Lizzie had gone, Fiona relieved her pent-up nerves with a hearty burst of tears. Then she dried her eyes and tried to think what to do about Penelope and her poet. Euphemia would be taken care of, it was easy to sponsor Letitia Helmsdale—but what would Cleveden say if he found his home being used for Penelope Buxtable's romance?

The Marquess of Cleveden's appointment was with a vicar who was on the board of one of his charities. Matters were soon dealt with, and as he made his way back to the West End he wondered what to do about Penelope Buxtable.

Was Fiona being forced to concern herself with the three ladies because that had threatened to tell him of the wager? And would Mrs. Buxtable go so far as to use his house to meet her lover?

The more he thought of his wife's worry and distress, the more convinced he became that her wager had led her into more trouble.

Instead of going home, he drove to the Cavalry Club and asked if Colonel Henry Buxtable was present. He was told the colonel was in the coffee room and made his way there.

Colonel Buxtable was a thin, tall leathery man with a long face and a stern, uncompromising mouth. The marquess had met him before and so was able to talk easily about mutual friends until the colonel fixed him with a hard bright eye and asked, "But what brings you here, Cleveden? White's is more your turf."

"I am here to see if I can talk you out of calling me out."

"But I haven't challenged you to a duel!"

"I think you might," said the marquess equably, "for I am about to interfere in your marriage. No, do not reach for your glove to strike me across the face until you have heard me out. Your excellent wife is a friend of my wife's. She is a most romantic lady."

"What! *Your* wife?"

"No, yours."

"Nonsense. That's what I admire in my Penelope. No rubbish."

"I agree Mrs. Buxtable is an extremely straightforward lady, but I fear she is being seduced by culture."

"By *who*?" demanded the colonel, beginning to turn a dangerous color.

"Culture. The arts, dear fellow. In short, poetry."

"Explain!"

"She has seen fit to offer her patronage to a young poet, one Peregrine Finlay."

The colonel visibly relaxed. "Oh, *him*," he said with a bark of laughter. "Perfect milksop. Had him to dinner. Man milliner. Weakling."

"Your wife spends a great deal of time in his company. For her part, she is completely innocent," said the marquess, who did not believe any such thing. "But this Finlay fellow—ah, there's another matter. If we are not careful, this weakling may start to create the idea he is having an affair with a married lady in order to give himself some much-needed cachet."

"That's enough, sirrah! You have gone too far."

"No, no," said the marquess soothingly, "you are not going to call me out. The reason you have not heard of this is that everyone is frightened to tell you anything for fear you put a ball through them."

"May I ask what concern this is of yours?"

The marquess leaned forward and tapped the colonel gently on the knee with his quizzing glass. "When your wife has got around *my* wife and made her agree to receive her and her poet in *my* house this afternoon, then it became my business."

The colonel looked about to rage, to fume, to curse, and then his long, thin body went limp and he leaned back in his chair and closed his eyes.

"Don't tell anyone, Cleveden," he said, "but things have been going badly wrong between myself and Penelope. I don't know what to do. I ain't one of those fellows that can force themselves on women."

"It depends on the woman," said the marquess. "I think your excellent lady would enjoy being dragged off by the hair. If things are as bad as you say, why not give it a try? My wife should never have agreed to have let the pair of them call on us this afternoon, but she is very young and not used to our decadent society. She is Highland, you know."

"Highlanders!" said the colonel. "Lot of Hottentots. Demned murdering savages."

"Now, if you go on like that, I shall have to call *you* out."

"Sorry," mumbled the colonel. "Rude of me. Upset. Don't know what to do."

The marquess leaned forward again. "Then, I'll tell you. . . ."

* * *

Fiona was in a fever of anxiety by the time three o'clock approached. She told Osborne no callers other than Mrs. Buxtable and Mr. Finlay were to be admitted.

She dreaded her husband's return, wondering how she could explain the presence of the poet, particularly if the bold Penelope made it obvious she was smitten by him.

On the stroke of three, Penelope arrived, highly painted and swathed in furs. Fiona thought gloomily that Penelope already looked like a member of the Fashionable Impure.

She was no sooner seated than Osborne announced Mr. Finlay. Fiona looked at the poet in amazement. He was a thin, weak creature with a nipped-in waist and enormous buckram-wadded shoulders. He stank like a civet cat and had that funny rolling sailor walk caused by the wearing of fixed spurs. His hair was teased and back-combed high on his head, giving his pale face a look of perpetual surprise, this effect being heightened by his shaved eyebrows. He promptly dropped down onto the carpet at Penelope's feet and began to lounge in quite the latest manner.

Fiona did not want to leave them alone. She gamely talked about the weather, Napoleon, the price of bread, until Penelope said with a meaningful look when she at last fell silent, "You seem to have exhausted all topics . . . except gambling," and gave a little jerk of her head toward the door.

Rising miserably to her feet, Fiona was about to

keep up appearances by thinking up an excuse for leaving the room when the door opened and the Marquess of Cleveden, accompanied by Colonel Henry Buxtable, walked in.

TWELVE

"Mrs. Buxtable!" said the colonel. "Come with me. I want to talk to you."

Mr. Finlay tried to leap to his feet from his lounging position, staggered over backward, fell over a backless sofa, and disappeared behind it.

Penelope's face flamed. "I am not going with you. I am staying here with Peregrine."

The colonel looked wildly at the marquess, who gave a little nod.

"In that case," gritted the colonel, "you are not the wife for me. If that weakling wants you, he can have you. I shall see him in court."

Peregrine Finlay leapt straight up from behind the sofa like a jack-in-the-box. His face was ashen. "I was only making a social call," he cried, "and happened to find Mrs. Buxtable here."

"Peregrine," said Penelope, aghast. "You *love* me!"

"No, I don't. No, I don't," squeaked Peregrine,

jumping up and down. "Never said I did." He turned to the colonel. "Splendid lady, your wife, sir, but got windmills in her head."

Penelope howled, "But that night at the opera, you said—"

"No, no, *no!*" screamed Peregrine. "Never did. Said nothing. Foxed. Oh, the deuce." And before anyone could guess what he was about to do, he sprang over the sofa and shot out of the drawing room into the hall. A second later the street door banged and the sound of frantically running feet disappearing in the distance could be heard.

"Now, madam," began the colonel.

"My love," said the marquess to Fiona, "I have something urgent to discuss with you."

Glad to escape, Fiona followed him from the room.

The marquess closed the drawing-room door. "Come into my study," he said.

They crossed the hall together. From behind them, from behind the closed door of the drawing room, came the crack of a slap and then the sound of noisy weeping.

"Oh, poor Colonel Buxtable," said Fiona. "Cannot you go to his aid? Penelope has slapped him."

"Leave them be. If I am not mistaken, the colonel has slapped Penelope. She is an extremely slappable woman."

They sat down together in the book-lined study. Fiona saw her husband was looking at her as if

Miss Fiona's Fancy

waiting for an explanation, so she said hurriedly, "Was it by chance that Colonel Buxtable came here?"

"The same chance that brought Mrs. Buxtable and Mr. Finlay together under my roof. Or did you arrange that?"

Fiona hung her head.

"You must not let your female friends impose on you. Now, what is all this about Letitia Helmsdale? You said something about sponsoring her."

"Yes, she so wants to get married. I fail to understand why she has not taken. She is extremely wealthy."

"It takes a great deal of good solid groundwork to puff off even an heiress. You had better leave it to me. We shall give a ball here at the start of the Little Season and do our best for her. But it would be tactful if I called on her parents and discussed the matter."

"Oh, you are very good," said Fiona, her eyes shining. Her brain worked rapidly. If only Penelope would come to her senses, that would leave only the problem of Euphemia.

"Now, I saw Lizzie Grant's card on a tray in the hall with the corner bent down, which means she called in person. Did you receive her?"

"I am afraid I did," said Fiona. "She will not call again."

"The call was not pleasant, I gather."

"Very unpleasant. My father called before Lizzie arrived and told me he thought Lizzie was trying to force him to gamble again. It is very easy to lure a gambler back to the tables by telling him of lucky signs and omens."

"Did you challenge her with this? And did she say why?"

"Yes. She hates me and wanted to hurt me through hurting my father. There is a reason for this, but I cannot tell you, Charles, because it involves a secret about Lizzie I promised the duchess not to tell anyone."

There was a short silence, then he said, "Have you inherited your father's penchant for cards and dice . . . and ridiculous bets?"

"I did like to gamble," said Fiona. "But after I saw what it could do, I decided never to play cards again, even for fun."

He looked at her in silence, his golden eyes searching her own, and she had a feeling he was waiting for more. Unless she distracted him, she would find herself telling him about that wager, and then he would not love her anymore. Perhaps he did not really love her, and still only found her amusing.

"How did your appointment go?" she asked.

"Very well. My love, as my wife I think you should know I spend a large amount of money on various charities to help the poor and orphaned."

"Oh, that is splendid," said Fiona. "Perhaps you might take me with you next time? I could find some way to be of assistance."

"It is not very pleasant work."

"At least it is useful work," sighed Fiona. "Balls and parties and dressing up are very hard work as well, but no one benefits."

"Then you shall come with me next time. What an odd female you are, Fiona! Tell me, what are your feelings now about my rival?"

"You have no rival, Charles."

"I mean that peculiar place you hail from . . . Strathglass."

Fiona laughed. "One does not fall in love with houses, Charles."

"Oh, but one does. Are you still homesick?"

"No. Not any longer."

"Why?"

She wanted to say because she loved him. But did he love her? Did he not want a light easy marriage that kept him amused without putting any heavy emotional burdens on him?

"Because it is more amusing here," she said with a little laugh that sounded silly and empty to her own ears.

He looked at her enigmatically and was about to say something when they heard the colonel and Penelope in the hall.

The marquess rose and opened the study door. Fiona peeped over his arm.

The colonel looked as proud as if he had just won some military campaign. He had an arm around his wife's waist and she drooped against his shoulder.

"Good day to you, Cleveden," called the colonel

cheerfully. "Got to be on our way. Come, my love."

"Yes, Henry," cooed Penelope, gazing tenderly up into his face.

"Well, that's that," said the marquess, shutting the study door again.

Fiona looked at him doubtfully. "Did you know about Penelope and Mr. Finlay, Charles?"

"Yes."

"And did you tell the colonel?"

"Not exactly."

"You seem to know a great amount of gossip, Charles."

"Oh, yes. As I told you before, it can be very useful. For example, while you were away, there was a very odd rumor circulating about that the Marchioness of Cleveden, while still Miss Fiona Grant, ran a gambling hell. I squashed that rumor, but how do you suppose such an odd tale got about?"

Fiona bit her lip. She was very aware that if Euphemia had told her parents she needed £3,000 to pay Miss Grant who ran a gambling hell, then it was possible the other two had told their parents the same story.

"No ideas?" he mocked as she remained silent. "Well, my love, it appears we have the rest of the day to ourselves. What would you like to do?"

All Fiona wanted to do was to be carried upstairs to his room, to sink into his bed and into his arms, and make love. She stood in front of him, her head bent, while he looked at the top of her curls.

"Let me see your face," he said softly.

She raised her head. Her mouth was swollen and her green eyes were almost black. "Charles..." she said, and put a timid hand on his sleeve.

"Charles," she tried again, "it is hard to be intimate with you when you are so *very* well dressed. That beautiful cravat is so starched and sculptured that—"

"Fiona," he said with a laugh, sweeping her up into his arms. "Simply clothes, nothing but clothes, and fine clothes can be taken off like any others."

They walked sedately from the study and up the winding staircase and along the corridor to his room. Once inside, he said simply, "Oh, Fiona. Love me."

They both fell on the bed, kissing each other as frantically as if they were shortly about to be parted. She kissed the hard planes of his face and sank her hands in the thick black mass of his hair.

He caught her full bottom lip between his teeth, and Fiona said in a choked voice, "Aren't you even going to remove your boots, Charles?"

"If only there were some way of getting clothes to melt," he muttered as he wrenched at his cravat and then fumbled with the tiny gold buttons on his waistcoat. Clothes then went flying over the room —boots, coat cravat, cambric shirt, leather breeches, muslin drawers to fall in an untidy heap, which was shortly augmented with a silk pelisse, a muslin gown with the tapes torn, two petticoats, a pair of flesh-colored stockings, two garters, and the very latest thing in ladies' drawers.

"Fiona," he muttered at last, his mouth against the nipple of her left breast, "let me know when it is morning."

Downstairs, callers came and callers went. Stately Osborne murmured that, yes, my lord and lady were at home but very much occupied, and abovestairs the great bed heaved and creaked as the Marquess and Marchioness of Cleveden wondered if they could ever have enough of each other.

Fiona awoke next day at ten in the morning to find her husband gone. She was ravenously hungry, as they had not bothered to eat dinner the night before, and no longer worried about shocking the servants, she pulled the blankets up to her throat, rang the bell, and ordered a hearty breakfast.

She was just finishing it when the marquess came back. He was dressed for riding.

"How on earth do you find the energy?" marveled Fiona. "I feel like going back to sleep."

"And so we shall." He yawned. "I went riding in the Row and met Harry—Harry Gore. He has a most odd piece of gossip."

"Which is?" asked Fiona, looking at her husband nervously.

"Why, that Lizzie Grant is the Duchess of Gordonstoun's natural daughter."

"Who would say such a thing!" cried Fiona out loud, but privately thinking, At least it was not I. My conscience is clear on that score.

"Well, here's an odd thing," he said, sitting down on the bed. "Harry is a tremendous gossip, but it's never malicious. He may rattle on to me in private, but if he has a piece of gossip that would harm anyone, he does not spread it about. The reason he told me, was because the source of the gossip was none other than Lizzie Grant herself. She sought him out to tell him. Did you know the identity of her mother?"

"Yes, Lizzie told me yesterday. I did not tell you, because I had promised the Duchess of Gordonstoun that I would never reveal Lizzie's illegitimate state. She is mad! She must have told Mr. Gore in the hope he would repeat it. Why? She has ruined her chances of marriage."

"Not she! Most people believed her to be illegitimate anyway. Members of the *ton* do not put their daughters into trade. But it is well known the duchess has quarreled bitterly with her two legitimate daughters and that she dotes on Lizzie. The duchess is a very rich woman, one of the richest in Britain. Lizzie has a better chance than ever of finding a husband. The world is cruel. To be plain Mrs. Bloggs's bastard child is a shame and disgrace. To be the illegitimate child of a rich and doting duchess is quite another. Clever Lizzie."

"It is amazing," said Fiona. "I was there, you know, when the duchess saw Lizzie for the first time since she gave birth to her. Not by one flicker of an eyelid did she show that Lizzie was her daughter."

"Lizzie may not be her only by-blow. Perhaps she has many sons and daughters spread out over England and is used to meeting them without a blush."

"Why does Lizzie still hate me so?"

"Malcontents like Lizzie blame the whole wide world and her hate must have a focus. I shall not let her harm you."

"She frightens me, nonetheless."

The marquess took the tray from her lap and put it on the floor. Then he slid over to lie on top of her, smiling down into her face.

"Oh, Charles," said Fiona, wide-eyed. "You can't mean to . . . Not *again*. Oh, Charles . . ."

It was fortunate for Fiona that her husband had to attend the House of Lords a day later, for it transpired that a very angry Euphemia and Letitia had called several times and were on the point, they told her, of sending a message to her husband to tell him about the wager.

"I don't know how you can be so cruel," said Fiona, feeling too tired and debilitated to cope with anything.

But the ladies were quickly cheered by her news; Letitia was delighted at the prospect of a ball, and said she was sure her parents would forget their prejudices against Fiona if the marquess called on them. Euphemia was relieved that Fiona was still set to go ahead with the arrangement for her elopement. Fiona only hoped she could get Euphemia safely away on her road north without her husband finding out about it. But Euphemia assured her that no one knew of her love for Captain Gaunt.

While Fiona entertained her friends, her husband was talking to Mr. Harry Gore in Parliament Square. Mr. Gore had waylaid his friend outside the House of Lords to see if the marquess would care to step along to White's for a game of hazard.

"No," said the marquess. "Having Sir Edward Grant as a father-in-law is enough to frighten one off gambling forever. But I shall walk along with you and we shall broach a bottle of port. Must you play?"

"I am low in funds and hope to repair my losses."

"My very dear Harry. There are other solutions —like sending me your bills."

"Never!"

"I am a safer bet than gambling or moneylenders. Still, there is perhaps another solution. Would you like to be married?"

"I suppose I shall marry eventually. There is no rush. I am not so long in the tooth as you."

"You are nearly thirty, my friend. Have you never seen a lady who would suit?"

Mr. Gore heaved a sigh. "They are all too *knowing* for me. Even a chit out of the schoolroom makes me feel like a callow youth. I shall never marry for money. If I can't afford to get married, then I won't."

"You want to look out for an heiress," said the marquess. "Someone very young and rather plain and a bit shy."

"If I find such a paragon, I shall let you know," said Mr. Gore. "But do not prose on about marriage. It makes my head ache."

As the time for Euphemia's elopement rushed upon her Fiona found she would have to ask her husband for money so that she might rent a traveling carriage from a livery stable. Then she would need to find a way to make sure he was out of the house on that all-important afternoon.

She asked the marquess if she could have some pin money. The marquess took her down to his bank and made arrangements for her to draw as much money as she wanted whenever she wished.

It was then that Fiona decided she must tell him about the wager—as soon as ever she became shot of Euphemia. He trusted her with money; he trusted her not to gamble it away. Such trust must be returned and she must be prepared to take the consequences.

The question of money having been taken care of, Fiona then turned her mind to the problem of getting him away on the all-important afternoon. It would be something that would have to take him away for several hours so that by the time Osborne reported she had driven off with an army captain, she would have fulfilled her obligations to Euphemia and would be returned home. "Tell him about the wager *now*," screamed a voice in her head, "and then you will not have to aid Euphemia in this silly elopement."

But in her heart of hearts she was deeply sorry for Euphemia. To be forced into marriage with an old man was a dreadful fate.

At last Fiona realized she would have to lie and she would have to involve Mr. Harry Gore in that lie.

The day before the elopement, Mr. Gore came to call. The marquess was not at home but expected back very soon, Fiona told him, and then pressed him to wait.

Steeling herself, she said, "Mr. Gore, I would like to buy my husband a present as a surprise. It is a very special present and it involves me going out of Town a little way tomorrow afternoon. Could you please try to get my husband to go away somewhere with you for several hours? If he finds me gone from home, he will worry. Do please say yes."

"It is very hard to make Cleveden go anywhere if he does not want to leave home—and he certainly does not want to stay away from home for very long since your return from the north."

"Oh, please," begged Fiona.

Mr. Gore thought it was all very romantic.

"I shall do my best, Lady Cleveden," he promised.

THIRTEEN

The plan seemed to be working well. Next day, the marquess said to Fiona, "I must leave you this afternoon. Harry Gore is in a state about some lady and is anxious I should meet her. She lives in Richmond. I cannot understand why we cannot all go, but I do not wish to press too hard for I have never known Harry show an interest in any female before."

"Oh, really." Fiona stretched and yawned and failed to see the sharp look of suspicion her husband cast on her.

"Harry spent some time alone with you yesterday," said the marquess. "Did he say nothing to you?"

"No," said Fiona. "But then he has not known me very long."

He swung his long legs out of bed. "Go along to your room, my love," he said, "so that Gustave may shave me."

Her senses dulled by another long night of lovemaking, Fiona did as she was bid and did not realize her husband was becoming more suspicious about the reason for the journey to Richmond by the minute. Her reaction to his news about Harry had been just *too* casual.

But once she was fully awake and dressed, all Fiona's anxieties and worries returned.

At half past two when Mr. Gore arrived and the marquess left with him a few moments afterward, Fiona could have wept with relief.

"What is the name of your fair lady?" asked the marquess, tooling his carriage through the traffic.

"Eh!" Mr. Gore started. "Helen! That's it. Mrs. Helen Peters."

"A widow?"

"Yes."

"And who was her husband?"

"A squire. Look, I am so nervous, I do not wish to talk about it anymore until you have seen her."

"My dear Harry, when we spoke of marriage only the other day, you gave me the impression that you had no one in mind."

"I've been working up to it," said Mr. Gore desperately. "Hit me all of a heap. Must get married. Why are you stopping?" For the marquess had reined in his team by the Bunch of Grapes in the Brompton Road.

"I think we should have a glass of wine to fortify ourselves for the coming visit."

"No time," said Mr. Gore. "Mrs. Baxter is expecting us."

"I thought her name was Mrs. Peters."

"Hyphenated. Baxter-Peters."

"Step down, Harry," said the marquess. "You have some explaining to do."

At three o'clock, Lizzie Grant was walking along Curzon Street with her maid. She often walked down Curzon Street, drawn always to the house where Fiona lived.

Lizzie's hatred of Fiona had started at an early age.

As a little girl, Fiona had been brought on a visit to Lord Charles Grant's home. Lizzie, a little girl herself, was already expected to help about the house, not make a noise, and not do anything to bring herself to the attention of her betters.

Lizzie could not help contrasting her own state with that of this legitimate daughter of the Grant family. The first thing that burned most into Lizzie's soul was that Fiona was wearing new shoes, shiny shoes with silver buckles, while she, Lizzie, went barefoot. So although there were other members of the Grant family she could have turned her hatred on—her father, for instance—all the loathing for her bastard state was turned on Fiona. Although she never saw her again until the day at the dressmaker's, Lizzie's hatred was as fresh as ever. She had found out, by picking the lock on her father's desk and reading his correspondence, the identity of her mother. Had the duchess not called at South Molton Street and then arranged to take her under her wing, Lizzie would have called on her and threatened her with exposure if she had not accepted her. As it was, with the duchess fondly doing everything for her, Lizzie had her full trust and had been able to disassociate the duchess's affections from her other two daughters. The success of this manipulation had gone to her head. She was still sure there was something to do to harm Fiona. She even prayed nightly to be given such a chance, confident that her hatred was right and just.

And so the sight that met her eyes outside the marquess's town house seemed like an answer to her prayers.

For there was Fiona, climbing into a rented traveling carriage with an army captain. They looked furtive and secretive. There were no grooms or outriders, no maid. None of the trappings of a marchioness setting out on a journey.

There was only a sour-looking coachman in shabby livery on the box.

As soon as the carriage had driven out of sight, Lizzie crossed the road and banged on the knocker.

When Osborne answered the door, she asked for the Marquess of Cleveden.

"His lordship is gone from home," said Osborne stiffly.

"I shall await his return," said Lizzie brightly.

"That will not be necessary," declared Osborne.

"But the Duchess of Gordonstoun is anxious to see his lordship and will be joining me."

Osborne hesitated. He had been told not to admit Lizzie unless she was accompanied by the duchess. But if the duchess was coming . . .

He stood aside to let Lizzie past. With quite the air of the lady of the house, Lizzie ordered tea. She could sense the restless air of the house and hear the servants gossiping feverishly to each other.

When a footman came in with the tea tray, Lizzie said, "How odd of dear Lady Cleveden to dash off in only a hired carriage."

"Yes, miss," said the footman stonily. "Will there be anything else?"

Lizzie took two guineas from her reticule and held them up so that they winked in the light. "I am deeply concerned for the welfare of Lady Cleveden and fear she has done something dangerous. Would you know where that carriage was bound?"

The footman was young and only the fourth footman. He thought what he could do with those two guineas.

He held out his hand. "Mr. Osborne felt it his duty to find out from the coachman where the carriage was bound," he whispered.

Lizzie held the guineas out toward him. "And where was that?"

"Gretna."

Lizzie sighed with pure pleasure and handed over the money.

The servants would undoubtedly tell their master where his wife had gone. But Lizzie wanted to be the first to tell him, to see the fury on his face, and then pray he caught up with Fiona on the road.

"Now, Harry," said the marquess as his team trotted briskly homeward, "you should have told me the truth in the first place. My wife is up to something. She could easily have bought me a present when she was out shopping, and I do not believe this fairy story of her having to go out of Town to get it."

"I never could keep a secret," said Mr. Gore miserably.

"Well, you might have kept it if you had thought up a more intelligent excuse," said the marquess heartlessly.

He shouted to his tiger to hold the horses and strode into his home, followed by Mr. Gore.

Lizzie Grant rushed into the hall to meet him.

"What are you doing here?" snapped the marquess.

"Miss Grant said she was waiting for the Duchess of Gordonstoun to join her," said Osborne hurriedly.

"But listen!" cried Lizzie. "The most terrible news, my lord. Fiona has run off to Gretna with a captain."

"Osborne!" demanded the marquess. "Is this true?"

"For some reason my lady has gone off in a hired traveling carriage which the rented coachman said was bound for Gretna."

"The name of this captain?"

"Captain Peter Gaunt."

"And you let her go?"

"It is not my place to stop my lady, my lord," said Osborne.

"You made a great mistake in marrying her, Cleveden!" cried Lizzie. "I tried to warn you before—"

"Silence, woman," roared the marquess, and Lizzie fell back in fright and clutched her maid for support. "I love Fiona and do not believe she has run off with anyone. I think she is up to some mad escapade. Come, Harry. Miss Grant, you may tell the Duchess of Gordonstoun to expect me on my return. There are certain facets of your fascinating little personality of which I feel sure she should be made aware."

"Is this all the thanks I get for trying to help you, my lord?" said Lizzie, beginning to cry.

"You hate my wife. You blame her for your bastard status. You are quite mad, in my opinion. If your illegitimate birth galls you so much, then I suggest you turn your hatred on your mother. Get out!"

Lizzie scurried off. The marquess said to Mr. Gore, "I had better set off in pursuit. Goodness knows what mess she is in."

And then in came Miss Letitia Helmsdale followed by her faithful maid.

"What do you want?" barked the marquess.

"I came to see if Lady Cleveden has returned," said poor Letitia, whose strong point had never been geography, either global or local, and was under the impression that Barnet was somewhere over in the City.

"Returned from where?" said the marquess, looking at her with sharp suspicion.

Letitia started in alarm. If she said Fiona was only helping Euphemia to elope, then this awe-inspiring husband of hers might dash off to Euphemia's parents and all poor Fiona's work would go for naught. Perhaps he might even learn how they had coerced his wife into helping them, and then she would never have that ball. She decided to remain silent.

"I had better go," she said, edging toward the door.

"Stay right where you are," ordered the marquess. Letitia began to cry. Never a pretty girl, Letitia looked at her worst as she stood there, sobbing helplessly. Mr. Gore's kind heart was touched.

"I say," he said awkwardly. "We are wasting time. Nothing to do with Miss Helmsdale. Let's go."

"If I find you have had anything to do with this, Letitia Helmsdale," raged the marquess, "I shall wring your neck."

Mr. Gore placed himself between the marquess and Letitia. "You shall not speak to her thus!" he cried.

"I do not care what you say, Harry," said the marquess. "I feel sure she has something to do with this and she is coming with us."

He urged them toward the door. "No, Harry,"

said the marquess firmly as Mr. Gore tried to drag Letitia back. "If I am wrong in taking Miss Helmsdale, then you may call me out when we return. Come along. Miss Helmsdale, there is no room for your maid. Leave her!"

Mr. Gore decided it would be better for Miss Helmsdale if he gave in. He had never seen his friend, the marquess, in such a savage temper and his soft heart was touched by Letitia's distress.

Sobbing into a handkerchief, Letitia was made to sit bodkin between the marquess and Mr. Gore.

She was to remember that journey as the most frightening of her life. The marquess drove like a man possessed. Buildings flew past on either side; they overtook other carriages on the road with barely an inch to spare. Letitia thought they were all about to be killed and buried her face in Mr. Gore's chest while he put a protective arm around her. She thought if they were not killed, and the guilty parties were not at Barnet, then the marquess might speed on all the way to the Scottish borders without stopping.

At Barnet, Fiona kissed Euphemia good-bye. She looked so radiant as she ran into her captain's arms that Fiona's conscience was eased. Two people so much in love deserved to be together.

She waved the happy couple good-bye and then returned to the hired postchaise that Euphemia had used to convey her to Barnet.

"Someone do be in a tearing hurry," remarked the driver of the postchaise laconically.

Fiona stood with one foot on the step of the postchaise and, with a sinking heart, watched the arrival of her husband with Mr. Gore and Letitia.

"Wait," she said to the driver. She walked forward to meet them.

"Charles," she said pleadingly. "I can explain everything."

"I never told him *anything*," said Letitia bravely, although she clutched onto Mr. Gore for support.

"I am not going to have explanations out in the street," said the marquess. He called to an ostler who was standing outside the White Falcon posting house to see to the horses. Then while Mr. Gore tenderly lifted Letitia down, he told the driver of the postchaise to make himself comfortable until he was needed and tossed him a crown.

With the small party of Fiona, Letitia, and Mr. Gore trailing after him, he marched into the posting house and demanded not one, but two private parlors.

"Take Miss Helmsdale off, Harry," said the marquess curtly. "I shall see her later."

Then he turned to his dejected wife. "*Now*, Fiona. Follow me."

Fiona silently followed him upstairs and into a private parlor.

"Wait," ordered the marquess when she was about to speak. He rang the bell and ordered wine and waited until the servant had left.

He poured two glasses and then leaned back in a chair at the table and faced Fiona who was sitting at the other end. "You may begin," he said.

"I was helping Euphemia Perkins to elope with a certain Captain Peter Gaunt. She was being forced by her parents to marry an old man, and, oh, she does love her captain so."

"Why did you not tell me your plans? Why did you cause such a scandal? You must know our servants would question that hired coachman and be told you were bound for Gretna."

Fiona hung her head. "You see, I am not accustomed to arranging elopements," she said.

"I cannot understand love without trust, Fiona."

"Oh, Charles," said Fiona, "I should have told you this a long time ago. Papa was deeply in debt. I made a bet with Letitia Helmsdale, Penelope Buxtable, and Euphemia Perkins that I could get you to propose to me. The bet was nicknamed Miss Fiona's Fancy. I did not mean to marry you. It sounds terrible now, but you did not seem to love me. You said you were marrying me because I amused you. I did not think you would be heartbroken. I was going to tell you the engagement was at an end, but Papa lost all the money. I knew I had to marry you. The nine thousand pounds I gained from the wager was not enough."

He looked at her bleakly. "This still does not explain why you helped Miss Perkins elope without telling me."

Fiona looked at him entreatingly, but his face was hard and set, the face of a stranger.

"The day after I returned from Scotland, the three came to see me. They said if I did not help them, then they would tell you of the bet. I should have told you. I meant to tell you, this evening, after Euphemia was safely away."

"Why not before?"

"I thought you would disapprove and try to stop me."

"Possibly I would. I would have gone to see Miss Perkins's parents and tried to talk some sense into their heads. But why did you not tell me of the wager in the first place?"

Fiona sat silently while he watched her narrowly. "When I thought you had married me for a whim, I did not think it necessary to tell you," she said in a low voice. "Then I fell in love with you, and I was terrified of losing your love, and that made me even more frightened of you finding out. When you trusted me with money, I felt the time had come to return that trust, no matter what it cost me. I did plan to tell you this evening."

"Why did you need money? Did you spend all the nine thousand pounds?"

"I have it still. I meant to take it to Scotland and perhaps spend it on improvements to my home. You gave me enough money for the journey, and when I looked at my money, the money I won, I could not bear to touch it."

"Fiona, I am a very rich man, but did it never

cross your head or did not those feckless parents of yours think to tell you that fifty thousand pounds was an enormous sum for a man to pay to marry into a penniless Highland family?"

"No," said Fiona miserably. "I fear we Grants do not know the value of money."

"And why do you think I packed you off to Scotland?"

"Because you were busy."

"I told you, it was to eliminate my rival . . . your home. So what do these actions tell you, my sweet?"

Fiona looked at him and saw the blaze of love in his eyes.

She clasped her hands. "Oh, Charles," she said. "Can it be that you truly love me?"

"Yes, idiot. Come here."

He rose to meet her as she flung herself into his arms. He smiled down at her tenderly. "I was beginning to have my good sense blinded by worry and jealousy and I am as silly as you. Two people cannot make love as much as we do just to pass the time of day. But I was sure you had not eloped with anyone. You see, my love, I knew of the wager all along. And I was sure this mad escapade of yours was connected with the three ladies involved in the bet."

"Charles! I have been so worried. How did you know of the wager?"

"Lizzie, of course. Lizzie scheming as usual. But if it had not been for Lizzie, I doubt if I would have troubled to see you again. It was when I learned I was Miss Fiona's Fancy that my interest was thoroughly caught. And that was why I asked you to meet me at the Pantheon. Oh, you were *so* arch and *so* missish, I wanted to see how far the gambling Miss Grant would go. But the duchess's eyes must be opened to Lizzie's true character."

"Poor Lizzie," sighed Fiona. "I have so much and she has so very little."

"Poor Lizzie stands to inherit a fortune."

"Not if you tell the duchess. And the duchess's other two daughters married well. They have no need of her money."

"Well, we shall see."

"Charles, why did you not tell me you knew of the wager?"

"I wanted you to tell me. I wanted all your love, all your trust. I love you so very much, Fiona."

He kissed her very slowly and sensuously until he felt her breath quicken. "Let us stay here for the night," he said. "I cannot wait until we get back to London."

"Oh, but Charles, what of Letitia? And Mr. Gore?"

"They will do very well without us. They can take that shabby postchaise back."

"I should see Letitia and comfort her. She was quite overset. Why did you drag her along?"

"I was worried, but not as furious as I appeared to be. I saw how my rage brought out the knight errant in Harry. *He* needs a rich wife and *she* wants a husband. Kiss me again, and let her tremble in fear a little longer."

Miss Fiona's Fancy

* * *

Letitia Helmsdale and Harry Gore sat in their private parlor and waited, and waited. Mr. Gore had listened, appalled, to Letitia's tale of the wager. He was sure the marquess would be breaking the inn furniture in his rage by now.

A silence had fallen between them. Letitia broke it by saying wretchedly, "They are taking a terribly long time."

"Odd," said Harry. "Only takes a few minutes to strangle your wife."

"Oh, poor Fiona," said Letitia, starting to cry again. "We should never have blackmailed her."

"Particularly not such a pretty little thing as you," said Mr. Gore gallantly. "Why, you will be married before the Little Season is over."

"No I won't," said Letitia. "M-men f-frighten m-me and if anyone l-looks interested in m-me, I *freeze* them."

"By George!" exclaimed Mr. Gore. "Ain't that the weirdest coincidence! The ladies frighten *me* to flinders."

Letitia was sitting on a small sofa at the window. He got up, went over, and sat down beside her. With great daring, he took her hand. "Seems we have a great deal in common," he said.

The Marquess of Cleveden, carrying his wife in his arms up to the bedchamber he had just ordered, stopped outside the parlor door and listened. Then he shouted at the top of his voice, "Just wait till I get my hands on that Helmsdale female. I'll kill her!"

Letitia cast herself into Mr. Gore's arms. All at once, Mr. Gore felt as strong as Hercules. "He shall not touch you," he said bravely. "Come, look up at me and smile."

She looked up at him, lips trembling, eyes red with crying.

It seemed the most natural thing in the world to kiss her. It was such a pleasant sensation that Mr. Gore decided he wanted more of it. Half an hour later, Letitia was sitting on his knee with her arms around his neck and her bonnet cast on the floor.

"Do you really want to marry me?" she asked shyly.

"Yes," said Mr. Gore in a dazed and happy way, thinking of a lifetime of kisses.

"It is very quiet," whispered Letitia. "I feel awfully brave now. Perhaps we should find out what has happened to poor Fiona."

Mr. Gore rang the bell. The landlord answered it in person. "Please convey my compliments to Lord Cleveden and tell him we are returning to Town," said Mr. Gore.

"His lordship said as how he was not to be disturbed."

"Where is he?"

"Gone to bed with his lady," said the landlord, drooping one eyelid in a wink. "Hugging and kissing they was."

Mr. Gore haughtily dismissed the landlord and turned to Letitia. "See, they are reconciled, and we have been worrying ourselves to pieces about nothing. I had better go with you to your parents as soon as we get back. I'll think of something to say. Your maid must have told them you were abducted by the Marquess of Cleveden!"

"There they go," said the marquess, standing at the bedroom window, "hand in hand to the post-chaise."

"Come away from the window, Charles! You are stark naked," said Fiona.

"And so are you," he said, returning to the bed. "We are all gamblers, Fiona. I gambled on winning your love and I won. At least I think I won. Love me again!"

FOURTEEN

"And what," said the Duchess of Gordonstoun frostily, "gives you the right to interfere in my affairs, Cleveden?"

It was a week after Euphemia's elopement and the marquess was not in the best of tempers. He had had to soothe down Euphemia's parents, persuade Letitia's parents that they were lucky to secure Mr. Gore as a future son-in-law, and crush the rumor that his own wife had run off to Gretna.

"Because your natural daughter, Lizzie, has seen fit to meddle in *my* affairs," he said testily.

"Ah, so you know Lizzie is my daughter?"

"Thanks to Lizzie the whole of the *ton* knows she is your daughter. She has seen fit on two occasions to try to turn Fiona against me. She has once, with success, persuaded Sir Edward Grant to gamble heavily and nearly succeeded the second time. Her hatred for my wife is insane. It is based on an unnatural jealousy. I wish her to be kept away from my home."

"Bastards are always touchy," said the duchess with apparently supreme indifference.

"That is putting it mildly," said the marquess, surprised. "It is rumored you do not speak to your own two legitimate daughters."

"Who said *they* were legitimate," said the little duchess with a shrug.

"My dear lady, if that is the case, why did you give two your name and yet neglect Lizzie for so long?"

"It was her father's fault, Lord Charles. He did not want his wife to find out. He told her the baby was Sir Edward's. My late husband could not father children and turned a blind eye to my little affairs."

"I was feeling sorry for you because I thought Lizzie was tricking you. But, may I say so, madam, you seem as bad as your daughter."

"There is nothing wrong with Lizzie that marriage will not cure. She is to wed Lord Blackburn."

"She is flying high."

"Lord Blackburn needs money for his estates in Yorkshire. I put marriage to Lizzie to him as a business proposition. He accepted on the understanding she would stay with him in Yorkshire. He does not like London. You will not be troubled by Lizzie."

"So Lizzie is not to be punished for her spite?"

"She will punish herself," sighed the duchess.

"Do not worry. She will not trouble Fiona again. What a tiresome conversation we are having. Do talk about something more amusing...."

"And that," said the marquess to Fiona an hour later, "is that. And they call men immoral."

"I cannot help still feeling sorry for Lizzie," said Fiona. "Perhaps she will forget all about me when she is married."

"I doubt it," said the marquess, "but since she is to reside in Yorkshire, I do not think she will have much opportunity to plague you again. Now, as to our honeymoon..."

"Oh, we are to have one after all."

"Especially after all. Do you wish to see your home again?"

"With you?"

"I had not thought to spend my honeymoon by myself."

"Oh, Charles, I would like it above all things."

"You may take your nine thousand pounds and use it to refurbish your home. Your tales of the kitchen are quite horrendous."

"I think I would rather give it to one of your charities. It would make me feel more... comfortable."

"Then you shall hand it over personally. Now what is making you look worried?"

"I do not know what you will make of my home or the Highlands of Scotland."

"Liar. You are worried because you do not know what your servants and tenants will make of this Englishman you have married."

"Well, they do not like the English much."

"We shall see. Scotland it is. With Napoleon controlling most of Europe, there are a limited amount of places to go."

But as their carriage finally rumbled along the broken roads of Inverness-shire, Fiona's misgivings grew. Her husband sat in the opposite corner of the carriage, fast asleep. She looked out at the countryside and felt she was seeing it through his eyes: the poverty, the barefoot children playing in the dirt beside the cottage doors, and the houses without chimneys where the smoke found its way out through holes in the turf roofs.

They were approaching Inverness when Fiona saw a band of tinkers camped out under a stand of trees beside the road. The marquess awoke as she called the coachman to stop.

"What is the matter?" he demanded.

"Tinkers. Gypsies. I wonder if they have news of Polly."

"They look quite frightening," said the marquess languidly. "I had better come with you."

"No," said Fiona, "you might frighten *them*." But the marquess climbed down from the carriage and stood watching as she went up to them.

Trying not to choke at the filthy smell of the gypsies, Fiona asked them if they knew of an English girl called Polly.

They stared at her sullenly. Fiona switched to

Gaelic and asked the same question. A heavyset man pushed his way forward.

"That'll be Johnny Gray's girl," he said. "Dead by now, maybe."

"What happened?" gasped Fiona.

"Caught pinching folks' handkerchiefs at the fair in Inverness. She stands trial at the sheriff court in Inverness today. Probably swing fer it."

Fiona turned around and looked at the marquess. He saw the distress in her face and came quickly to her side.

"It is Polly!" cried Fiona. "She is too stand trial at the sheriff court in Inverness today, and may even be already hanged. We must go."

"Very well," he said. "Has she been stealing handkerchiefs again?"

"Yes, Charles. But for all we know, she may be innocent."

The carriage could not move fast enough for Fiona as they set out on the road to Inverness, the marquess pointing out he was not going to have the whip laid on the backs of his hired horses.

"And when we arrive," he said, "stay in the carriage and leave the matter to me."

"But what if poor Polly has been hanged?"

"If sentence has been passed, then she is probably in prison in the Tolbooth. They would hardly take her straight from the court to the gallows. If I thought her sentence might only be imprisonment, I would not interfere. I do not think Polly will ever stop thieving unless she gets a fright."

When they reached the sheriff court, Fiona made to get out of the carriage, but he held her back.

"You must wait," he said. "I can probably help Polly better on my own."

So Fiona waited. Two hours passed, and she was about to get out of the carriage when people began to flow out of the court. Then came her tall husband with a grimy bundle of rags behind him which she could just make out to be Polly.

The marquess thrust Polly into the carriage and climbed in after her. "Drive on quickly," he called to the coachman.

"How did you manage to free her?" asked Fiona. But the marquess said, "Later."

"I am ever so grateful, mum," whined Polly.

"And so you should be," said Fiona crossly. "Now you see what comes of stealing? You shall come home with me, Polly, and resume your training."

"Can't," said Polly. "Gotta see my husband."

"Polly, I am persuaded the gypsy life will be the death of you."

"Never bin so 'appy," said Polly. Then she broke into fluent Gaelic. "Besides, I am bearing his child. Please tell the man to stop. I must go."

Fiona called the driver, and the carriage rolled to a stop among a miserable collection of huts on the other side of the Inverness bridge.

Polly jumped down and stood grinning up at Fiona, hugging a dirty tartan shawl about her shoulders. "Bye, mum," she called. "Won't ever forget you."

She turned and scampered away through the houses.

"I had to let her go, Charles," said Fiona. "She is with child."

"Remarkably skinny for a pregnant girl," said the marquess cynically.

"How did you get her off?"

"To be frank with you, I nearly did not. I thought a term of imprisonment would do her good. But it transpired the sentence would almost definitely be hanging. So I talked to the witnesses and recompensed them for their lost handkerchiefs and pointed out the wicked sin of sending little more than a child to her death. So they refused to testify against her. She will not change, Fiona, and next time there will be no one to rescue her."

"People do change," said Fiona stoutly. "Only look at Papa."

After another two hours' journey, the coachman called down. "If this is your home, my lady, I cannot go any further. There are fallen trees over the drive."

The marquess swore gently under his breath. "We shall send all the menservants to maneuver the carriage up to the house," said Fiona. "We could also unhitch two of the horses and ride."

"Is it far?"

"No, not very far," said Fiona.

"Then we shall walk," said the marquess.

He jumped down and shouted orders to the servants to leave the carriage, unhitch the horses, and use them to help carry the baggage up to the house. He then took Fiona's arm and together they stumbled their way up the drive and over the fallen trees.

"Did your servants not know of our arrival?" asked the marquess.

"I did not think to write to them," said Fiona guiltily. "I am sure I did write. Oh, Charles, I think I left the letter unposted on my desk."

"That explains the trees," said the marquess. "It also considerably relieves my mind. I thought perhaps wild Highlanders were lying in ambush."

After some time, the marquess said, "It is very dark and we must have walked at least three miles."

"It is funny how memory tricks one," replied Fiona. "I always think of our house as being quite near the road. We are nearly there."

At last the black bulk of a large building loomed up in a clearing with a small moon riding high above its twisted chimneys.

Fiona pulled a frayed length of rope beside the door and a bell clanged out into the night.

"And who answers?" asked her weary husband. "The three witches?"

The door creaked open and a small wizened little man in a nightshirt stood on the threshold, a candle in his hand.

"It is I, Hamish," said Fiona. "Charles, this is

Hamish, our butler. Or rather, our butler while Dougal stays in London."

Hamish broke out into an angry flood of Gaelic. The marquess interrupted him, "Are we going to stand here in the cold all night? Let us in!"

Hamish backed off, muttering, and then walked around the great hall, lighting pine torches which were thrust in iron brackets in the walls. He shouted at the top of his voice and servants came rushing from all over, all in various stages of undress. They crowded around Fiona, cooing in Gaelic, hugging her, and exclaiming at the modishness of her gown. Then the various Grant poor relations descended from the attics in their nightwear and joined in the welcome.

Fiona held up her hands. "Silence!" she cried. "May I present my husband, the Marquess of Cleveden."

They all shuffled behind Fiona and stared at the marquess. He felt like an explorer being surveyed by a tribe of aborigines.

"My love," said the marquess, "is there any hope of supper and bed?"

Fiona cried orders in Gaelic and then drew the marquess over to the fire, which had just started to belch smoke out into the room. The various relatives crowded around and looked at the marquess in awe as if he were some rare beast. Fiona introduced them one by one—the maiden aunts, the half-pay captains.

The marquess was relieved to see that the long table was being hurriedly laid. A barrel of whisky was rolled in, and one by one the relatives shyly proposed toasts. After two hours of steady drinking, they were asked to seat themselves at the table. Roast venison, grouse, hare, and pheasant were carried in and then, to the marquess's amazement, all the servants sat down at the table as well, still in their nightwear.

When supper was over and the marquess was told by Fiona that they might retire, Hamish, the temporary butler, took off his nightcap and fished a letter out of it which he handed to the marquess, telling him it had arrived several days before. "And we wass about tae send it tae London, not knowing yourself wass coming," said Hamish, flashing an angry look at Fiona to show he had still not forgiven her for her unannounced arrival.

"I shall read it upstairs," said the marquess. "Lead the way, my sweeting."

Fiona led the way up the great stone staircase. "Hamish says the best bedroom has been prepared for us," she said, opening a massive door on the first landing. The room was bare, uncarpeted, and furnished with a few rickety tables and a great, lumpy bed. The fire consisted of a black mass of smoking peat.

Fiona started to apologize, but the marquess said, "I am so weary, I could sleep anywhere." He examined the seal on the letter and said, "This is from your father."

He read the contents and then sighed and passed the letter to Fiona.

Fiona read it in growing horror. Her father had

gambled again. In order to settle his debts, he had borrowed money from a moneylender and had given the name of the Marquess of Cleveden. He hoped his dear son-in-law would settle same debt and be assured that his affectionate father-in-law would never, ever gamble again. London was a wicked place. Sir Edward and Lady Grant were setting out for Scotland.

"Oh, Charles," said Fiona, beginning to cry. "I am so ashamed. Does no one change? First Polly and now Papa."

The marquess looked at his sobbing wife and said gently, "Come to bed, my love, and there we may be grateful that some things do not change—such as our love for each other."

At one point during the night, the marquess awoke choking as smoke filled the room. He opened the shutters and an icy gale blew straight in on his naked body. "No glass," he said. "No glass on the windows. I am fallen among savages."

His wife stirred in the bed behind him. The blankets fell from her shoulders to expose her breasts. Perhaps I am the savage, thought the marquess with a smile as he climbed back into bed and roused his wife for another session of energetic lovemaking.

He awoke in the morning, convinced someone was being slowly murdered under the window. He looked for a bell, and finding none, he went to the door and shouted. Hamish appeared, still in his nightgown.

"What is that noise?" demanded the marquess.

"Oh, that's Angus Robertson, the piper," said Hamish. "His chieftain was journeying to Inverness through the night when a traveler on the road told him you had arrived. The chieftain said that Angus and his wife might stay with you for the length of your visit. My, but it's a bonny sound."

The marquess closed the door and went back to the window. Angus was strutting up and down below, playing for all he was worth. Fiona struggled awake. "What beautiful piping," she said. "It must be Angus. No one else can play like that."

"No one," agreed her husband fervently, his mind busy with plans. Glass for the upper windows and encourage Angus to go and play somewhere else. A builder to see to the chimneys.

"I have everything I want," said Fiona dreamily. "You, my home, Angus and Christine . . . oh, if only Papa would not gamble."

He slid back into bed beside her. "If you had not a gambler's blood in your veins and you had not made that silly wager, I might not have married you, and oh, that does not bear thinking of."

He put his arms around her and buried his face in her breast.

"Breakfast!" shouted a cheerful voice.

The marquess straightened up, holding Fiona against him.

Hamish came in with a heavy tray, which he balanced on top of their bodies. "Breakfast in bed Christine Grant—I mean her that's now Christine

Robertson—said. So here it is. Spoiling yourselfs, that's what you're doing."

"Get out of here immediately, you cheeky old man," shouted Fiona.

Hamish began to whine back in Gaelic.

The marquess started to eat his breakfast. He would leave the handling of these peculiar servants to his wife until he learned how best to deal with them himself. If Osborne had behaved in such a way, the marquess would have thrown his boots at him.

If he could suffer Sir Edward as a father-in-law, then he could put up with anything. He placidly ate his breakfast and let the battle rage over his head.

About the Author

Born in Glasgow, Scotland, Ms. Chesney started her writing career while working as a fiction buyer in a bookstore in Glasgow. She doubled as a theater critic, newspaper reporter, and editor before coming to the United States in 1971. She later returned to London, where she lives with her husband and one child near Kensington Palace.

ROMANTIC INTERLUDES

- [ ] THE DEMON RAKE by Gayle Buck (146093—$2.50)
- [ ] THE CLERGYMAN'S DAUGHTER by Julia Jeffries (146115—$2.50)
- [ ] THE CLOISONNE LOCKET by Barbara Hazard (145658—$2.50)
- [ ] THE WOOD NYMPH by Mary Balogh (146506—$2.50)
- [ ] THE HEIRS OF BELAIR by Ellen Fitzgerald (146514—$2.50)
- [ ] THE DUKE'S GAMBIT by Roberta Eckert (146522—$2.50)
- [ ] THE MARQUIS TAKES A BRIDE by Marion Chesney (146530—$2.50)
- [ ] LADY JANE'S RIBBONS by Sandra Heath (147049—$2.50)
- [ ] THE MAKESHIFT MARRIAGE by Sandra Heath (147073—$2.50)
- [ ] FASHION'S LADY by Sandra Heath (149130—$2.50)
- [ ] THE WICKED WAGER by Margaret Summerville (147057—$2.50)
- [ ] MISTRESS OF THE HUNT by Amanda Scott (147065—$2.50)
- [ ] THE RELUCTANT RAKE by Jane Ashford (148088—$2.50)
- [ ] THE FALSE FIANCEE by Emma Lange (148118—$2.50)
- [ ] THE PROUD VISCOUNT by Laura Matthews (148096—$2.50)
- [ ] A VERY PROPER WIDOW by Laura Matthews (148126—$2.50)

Buy them at your local bookstore or use coupon on next page for ordering.

⓪ SIGNET REGENCY ROMANCE (0451)

The Reign of Love

- ☐ THE NONPAREIL by Dawn Lindsey. (141172—$2.50)
- ☐ THE GREAT LADY TONY by Dawn Lindsey. (143825—$2.50)
- ☐ THE INCORRIGIBLE RAKE by Sheila Walsh. (131940—$2.50)*
- ☐ THE DIAMOND WATERFALL by Sheila Walsh. (128753—$2.25)*
- ☐ THE RUNAWAY BRIDE by Sheila Walsh. (138880—$2.50)
- ☐ THE INCOMPARABLE MISS BRADY by Sheila Walsh. (135687—$2.50)*
- ☐ THE ROSE DOMINO by Sheila Walsh. (136616—$2.50)*
- ☐ LORD GILMORE'S BRIDE by Sheila Walsh. (135229—$2.50)*
- ☐ THE PINK PARASOL by Sheila Walsh. (134796—$2.50)*
- ☐ THE GOLDEN SONGBIRD by Sheila Walsh. (141601—$2.50)†
- ☐ THE UNLIKELY RIVALS by Megan Daniel. (142098—$2.50)*
- ☐ THE RELUCTANT SUITOR by Megan Daniel. (096711—$1.95)*
- ☐ AMELIA by Megan Daniel. (142128—$2.50)

*Prices slightly higher in Canada
†Not available in Canada

Buy them at your local bookstore or use this convenient coupon for ordering.

NEW AMERICAN LIBRARY
P.O. Box 999, Bergenfield, New Jersey 07621

Please send me the books I have checked above. I am enclosing $_____
(please add $1.00 to this order to cover postage and handling). Send check or money order—no cash or C.O.D.'s. Prices and numbers are subject to change without notice.

Name _____

Address _____

City_____ State_____ Zip Code_____

Allow 4-6 weeks for delivery.
This offer is subject to withdrawal without notice.

SIGNET REGENCY ROMANCE (0451)

DUELS OF THE HEART

- ☐ LORD CLEARY'S REVENGE by Miranda Cameron (137620—$2.50)*
- ☐ THE MEDDLESOME HEIRESS by Miranda Cameron (126165—$2.25)*
- ☐ BORROWED PLUMES by Roseleen Milne (098110—$2.25)†
- ☐ MARCHMAN'S LADY by Caroline Brooks (141164—$2.50)*
- ☐ THE RUNAWAY PRINCESS BY Caroline Brooks (147804—$2.50)
- ☐ VENETIAN MASQUERADE by Ellen Fitzgerald (147782—$2.50)
- ☐ TOWN TANGLE by Margaret Summerville (142268—$2.50)*
- ☐ HIGHLAND LADY by Margaret Summerville (138031—$2.50)*
- ☐ SCANDAL'S DAUGHTER by Margaret Summerville (132750—$2.50)*
- ☐ THE EARL'S INTRIGUE by Elizabeth Todd (128745—$2.25)*
- ☐ HAND OF FORTUNE by Corinna Cunliffe (137639—$2.50)*
- ☐ PLAY OF HEARTS by Corinna Cunliffe (141156—$2.50)*
- ☐ LORD GREYWELL'S DILEMMA by Laura Matthews (143507—$2.50)*
- ☐ A VERY PROPER WIDOW (148126—$2.50)
- ☐ THE PROUD VISCOUNT (148096—$2.50)
- ☐ THE SECRET BLUESTOCKING by Eileen Jackson (143590—$2.50)*
- ☐ THE IMPETUOUS TWIN by Irene Saunders (147790—$2.50)

*Prices slightly higher in Canada
†Not available in Canada

Buy them at your local bookstore or use coupon on next page for ordering.

Ⓢ SIGNET REGENCY ROMANCE (0451)

WILLFUL BEAUTIES, DASHING LORDS

- ☐ THE REPENTANT REBEL by Jane Ashford. (131959—$2.50)
- ☐ A RADICAL ARRANGEMENT by Jane Ashford. (125150—$2.25)
- ☐ THE MARCHINGTON SCANDAL by Jane Ashford. (142152—$2.50)
- ☐ THE THREE GRACES by Jane Ashford. (145844—$2.50)
- ☐ THE IRRESOLUTE RIVALS by Jane Ashford. (135199—$2.50)
- ☐ MY LADY DOMINO by Sandra Heath. (126149—$2.25)
- ☐ MALLY by Sandra Heath. (143469—$2.50)
- ☐ THE OPERA DANCER by Sandra Heath. (143531—$2.50)
- ☐ THE UNWILLING HEIRESS by Sandra Heath. (145208—$2.50)
- ☐ MANNERBY'S LADY by Sandra Heath. (144392—$2.50)
- ☐ THE SHERBORNE SAPPHIRES by Sandra Heath. (145860—$2.50)
- ☐ A PERFECT LIKELESS by Sandra Health. (135679—$2.50)
- ☐ THE CHADWICK RING by Julia Jefferies. (142276—$2.50)

Prices slightly higher in Canada.

Buy them at your local bookstore or use this convenient coupon for ordering.

NEW AMERICAN LIBRARY,
P.O. Box 999, Bergenfield, New Jersey 07621

Please send me the books I have checked above. I am enclosing $_____
(please add $1.00 to this order to cover postage and handling). Send check or money order—no cash or C.O.D.'s. Prices and numbers are subject to change without notice.

Name_____

Address_____

City_____State_____Zip Code_____

Allow 4-6 weeks for delivery.
This offer is subject to withdrawal without notice.